"I thought maybe you were running around playing Santa or something."

If she only knew. "I don't think he'd appreciate my horning in on his business, do you?"

"That's all right, Mathias," Jacq consoled. "I'm sure you do your best."

"Gee, thanks," he retorted dryly. "It gives 'damned with faint praise' a whole new meaning."

"Only when you're being compared to Santa Claus." Tilting her head to one side, she teased, "You would look fantastic in a red suit, however. No competition there."

He offered a lazy smile. "Most people who know me would agree. Though I suspect the red suit they have in mind comes with a tail, horns and a pitchfork."

Welcome to the last of our Simply the Best showcase! This month's recommended reading is **Her Secret Santa** by RITA® Award nominee Day Leclaire.

UPCOMING BOOKS BY DAY LECLAIRE:
March 1998 #3495 **The Twenty-Four-Hour Bride**
Whirlwind Weddings
Nick Colter can't forget the one night he spent with Dani Sheraton, nine months ago. Neither can Dani—their baby's arrival is, well…imminent. Within twenty-four hours of Nick's return, Dani finds herself a wife and a mother. Now all she has to do is teach her new husband about love!

June 1998 #3508 **The Boss, the Baby and the Angel**
Guardian Angels
Combine one match-making angel, a tiny baby and a cynical boss and you end up with trouble made in paradise. Angie Makepiece is sent to earth to find Reed Harding a wife. Instead she finds something she's never experienced in heaven—or on earth—true love!

Fall 1998 **The Miracle Wife**
River Sierra wants a mother—a mother just like the beautiful fairy in her story-book. And so she makes a wish, a wish heard by her best friend—Gem. And, even if it takes a miracle, Gem's determined to find River a mother and Raven a wife!

This is a wonderful complete romance in itself, which also offers a unique opportunity to revisit old friends from **Her Secret Santa** (JJ) and **The Twenty-Four-Hour Bride** (Raven, River and Gem).

Her Secret Santa
Day Leclaire

Harlequin Books

TORONTO • NEW YORK • LONDON
AMSTERDAM • PARIS • SYDNEY • HAMBURG
STOCKHOLM • ATHENS • TOKYO • MILAN
MADRID • WARSAW • BUDAPEST • AUCKLAND

For Michelle Carew and all those who have fought her fight. May she inspire others as she inspired me. And special thanks to Katosha Belvin, Media Coordinator, National Marrow Donor Program.

ISBN 0-373-03486-5

HER SECRET SANTA

First North American Publication 1997.

Copyright © 1997 by Day Totton Smith.

Printed in U.S.A.

PROLOGUE

HE'D found her!

Mathias Blackstone allowed a small smile of satisfaction to touch his mouth. After all these months, he'd finally found Jacq Randell. The discovery brought him within one short step of his goal—to prove that the elusive Ms. Randell was the even more elusive Jack Rabbitt, author and illustrator of the most popular line of children's books currently on the market. His client would be pleased to hear the news.

Very pleased.

How interesting that he'd run her to ground in Seattle of all places, hiding right beneath his very nose. The fact that she'd turned out to be Turk Randell's daughter was even more ironic. Turk's public relations firm had been attempting to snag his attention for two solid years. It was a coincidence Mathias intended to use to his full advantage—once he came up with a client in need of a PR firm. Did Randell know his daughter was also Jack Rabbit? If not, it offered interesting possibilities.

After all the research he'd done, he was intensely curious to meet Jacq, which was why he'd accepted Turk Randell's invitation to this party. Mathias had hoped to meet her in an informal setting. The sketchy facts he'd gathered had captivated him, stirring an interest he hadn't felt in years. Studying her artwork—assuming it was hers—had only served to magnify that interest. She was twenty-eight, described by those who knew her as both strong and dainty, brilliant and vague, stubborn and easygoing. The contrasting comments intrigued him. Only on one fact did all agree. Jacq Randell guarded her privacy with ruthless determination.

He folded his arms across his chest and waited patiently until the glittering array of guests cleared from his line of vision. He'd been forced to ask someone to point her out, but fortunately such a large party allowed him to maintain a certain level of anonymity. It gave him time to analyze the situation at his leisure, while searching for any vulnerabilities he could use. As the tide of humanity finally ebbed, he spotted Jacq by the buffet table and fought a sense of amazement.

He found it hard to believe that this bit of whimsy was Turk Randell's daughter. She looked nothing like her father. For that matter, she didn't look anything like her brother or sister, either. To a one they exuded a brittle sophistication—tall and handsome with sleek black hair, sleeker figures and brilliant jet-hued eyes.

But not Jacq.

She was as delicate as spun glass. Almost coltishly slender, she'd caught the weighty mass of streaked blond curls at the nape of her long fragile neck. As she bent to sample the hors d'oeuvres, her scoop-necked dress revealed the fine bones of her shoulders and offered a tantalizing glimpse of sweetly rounded breasts. His mouth tightened. Didn't they ever feed the woman? Apparently not, considering the way she devoured the bite-size appetizers, her greed as unconscious as that of a ravenous child. She peeked around just then, as though checking to see if any observed her voracity. Huge hazel eyes dominated her triangular face. They stared out at her surroundings with an avid curiosity so revealing, he longed to shield her from a world waiting to consume her.

And then it hit him.

He was the only one waiting to consume her. He was the one destined to hurt her.

Too bad, came the regretful thought. He hadn't felt this attracted to a woman in a long time. But as much as he might wish it otherwise, his client's need took precedence. There could be no doubt about how this chase would end. Like the rest of the Randells, this woodland sprite didn't stand a chance against him.

J.J. Randell caught her brother, Cord, by the arm. "You're not going to believe this!" she said in a gleeful undertone.

"What? What did I miss?"

"Mathias Blackstone is here." J.J. towed him toward their father. "No, no, you fool. Don't look. He'll see you."

"He came? Blackstone actually came?"

Turk Randell joined them, a broad grin spreading across his striking face. "Oh, he came, all right."

A sardonic expression gleamed deep in J.J.'s dark eyes. Her father was practically salivating over the unexpected coup. But then, why shouldn't he? He'd been striving to gain Blackstone's attention for two solid years. To have such a man connected with their public relations firm would be worth a fortune.

"The interesting question is...*why* did he come?" J.J. commented.

"What do you mean, why?" A frown marred Turk's chiseled features. "He must be interested in using Limelight International. What other explanation could there be?"

J.J. shook her head. "I don't think so. He's here for

a reason, all right. But not the one you'd hoped. Look who's snagged his attention.''

Like puppets on a string, her brother's and father's gaze swiveled from Blackstone to the source of his scrutiny....

Jacq.

''Damn.''

''We're sunk.''

''What the hell could he want with her?'' Turk complained. ''She doesn't even work for the company.''

''Not anymore,'' J.J. couldn't resist needling. She studied Blackstone, adding sagely, ''And I think his interest is obvious.''

Her father's brows jerked together. ''You can't mean he's— You don't seriously believe he'd want—'' He gritted his teeth. ''Don't be ridiculous!''

''Wait a second, Dad. I think J.J.'s right,'' Cord inserted. ''I think Blackstone wants Jacq. It's a man/woman type deal. You know?''

''Only too well. I'm fifty, not dead,'' Turk snapped. ''It just doesn't make sense. Why would a man of Blackstone's caliber want someone as artless as Jacq?''

J.J. smiled sadly. ''How can you say that? She looks and acts exactly like Mom.''

A momentary anguish flickered deep in Turk's black eyes. ''She is like your mother,'' he whispered. ''Isn't she?''

''And every bit as attractive in a pixieish sort of way.''

Turk's mouth firmed. ''You both think that's what he's after? You think he wants Jacq?''

''Without question,'' J.J. responded.

''Absolutely,'' Cord seconded.

Their father inclined his head. "In that case, let's make certain Mr. Blackstone gets what he wants."

Jacq examined the buffet table with unconcealed greed, popping something round and vaguely green in her mouth. Not bad. But then, considering she couldn't remember her last meal, she wasn't inclined to be choosy. In fact, if it hadn't been for severe hunger pangs, she'd never have ventured within a thousand miles of her father's public relation "do."

She risked a quick glance in Turk's direction and frowned, a shrimpy something-or-other halfway to her mouth. Uh-oh. No question about it. She'd chosen the worst possible party to crash. Her dear relatives—jungle cats to a one—were definitely on the prowl. They'd slunk to the far end of the room, amassing like black storm clouds, their joint gazes glued to... She craned to catch a peek and nearly choked on her shrimp.

Dear heavens! Had they completely lost their collective minds?

The source of their fascination had to be the most dangerously attractive man she'd ever seen in her entire life. Just a single glimpse made her itch to grab a sketch pad and set to work—from a safe distance, of course. Tall, beautifully proportioned and leanly muscled, his hair was a rich ebony. And his eyes... Even from across the room she could see that his eyes were an incredible shade of ice-green. They were cool—too cool for her taste—with a sharp intelligence that warned that he didn't miss a trick.

He turned that gaze in her direction just then and she froze, seeing the fire beneath the ice, sensed the power and determination that ruled his keen intellect. It was then that she realized how thoroughly she'd overestimated her relatives. They weren't jungle cats, but yapping scavengers, fighting over food scraps this lithe, dragonesque creature spurned. Whatever they wanted from him, they were way out of their league.

This was a man to be avoided at all costs.

The instant he turned his attention elsewhere, Jacq scooped a handful of hors d'oeuvres into a linen napkin and beat a hasty retreat. Limelight International hoped to get something from this man-dragon and the safest place for her was out of the line of fire. Besides, she couldn't wait to get to work. From the moment she'd glanced his way, a thousand images had leaped to mind, followed by a thousand story ideas—all inspired by this one man. She had to get to her studio.

Now.

"Mr. Blackstone." Turk greeted his guest with a meticulous blend of jovial friendliness and careful deference. "How kind of you to attend our little get-together."

Mathias inclined his head, his attention centered on Jacq's hurried exit. "Randell."

Turk noted Blackstone's interest. It would seem J.J. was right. Jacq had definitely captivated the man. Damn. Without question, that would complicate their situation. Knowing his eldest daughter, she'd make matters as difficult as possible. In fact, she had a singular talent for it.

"I hope your presence means you've decided at long last to utilize our firm," Turk said, determined to seize the opportunity at hand.

"Not quite. I've decided to give your firm a trial run."

Not as much of a concession as Turk had hoped, but still a definite coup. "I'm delighted to hear it. Might I suggest a meeting to discuss specifics?"

"Excellent suggestion." Mathias turned then and focused the full power of his pale green eyes on Turk. "Tomorrow evening at six would be convenient."

"Fine, fine. Shall we meet at your office or—"

"I'd prefer we meet here. I'd like to get acquainted with the rest of your family. Your *entire* family."

"Of...of course." *Damn*! It didn't take a genius to read the underlying message. Blackstone expected Jacq to be there. "You'll join us for dinner tomorrow?"

"I'm afraid that won't be possible. I have other plans."

"I see." For the first time in a dog's age, Turk found himself at a loss for words. Only thirty years' worth of experience dealing with difficult situations saved him now. "Tomorrow at six it is, then," he said, offering Blackstone his hand. "We look forward to meeting with you."

Mathias inclined his head. "And I look forward to meeting the rest of your family."

He departed without another word, leaving Turk cursing with equal virulence Blackstone's disconcerting personality and his daughter's contrary nature. Neither boded well for Limelight International's future.

CHAPTER ONE

"YOU have to come," J.J. wailed, pacing the library of the main house in long, frantic steps. "We promised Blackstone you would."

Jacq shrugged. "I guess you'll have to unpromise him. You know better than to make plans on my behalf." She selected the book she needed and turned, shooting her sister a cool look. "Especially without consulting me first."

"But, we couldn't ask," her sister argued. "Blackstone caught us by surprise with his request. He announced that the entire family had to be present at this meeting tonight and then walked off. Believe me, it didn't leave any room for discussion."

"I'm sure he meant the Limelight portion of the family," Jacq said, seizing on the probability with ill-concealed relief.

J.J. shook her head. "Not a chance. According to the information we've been able to gather, Mathias Blackstone is the most exacting man anyone has ever met. He made it clear that he expected all the Randells present tonight and that's what he meant."

Jacq frowned, wishing she knew enough about the man to argue the point. Unfortunately, she didn't. Besides, her sister might be only twenty-four, but she had the uncanny ability to assess a person's strong points and flaws with pinpoint accuracy. It was a skill Turk exploited with ruthless disregard. If J.J. said Mathias Blackstone expected all the Randells to show up, then chances were excellent that's what he meant. Jacq nibbled on her lower lip. The question she'd like answered was...*why*?

An image of rapacious green eyes leaped to mind—eyes that currently graced the fierce black dragon in her latest series of sketches. She'd planned on adding a dragon to her children's books for over a year now—she'd even written the story that would introduce him to her readers. But she'd never found the right model for such a dangerously elegant creature.

Until now.

She scowled at the plant book she held. The frustrating part was that she'd spent all of last night and half of this morning working on the project. But no matter how hard she'd tried, she'd been unable to get the dragon quite right. Even after dozens of sketches the essence of the beast continued to elude her.

"Jacq, please say you'll come. This is important."

"For you Limelighters, it's always important," Jacq retorted absently. Maybe it was the body. Mathias Blackstone had a lithe elegance about him. A grace to his movements that she'd had difficulty adapting to the larger, more cumbersome size of a dragon. Perhaps if she tried sketching him in flight it would work better.

"No, I mean this is *really* important. Dad's been working for two solid years to catch Blackstone's eye. He's...he's put a lot of money into the campaign."

That caught Jacq's attention. "How much money?" she questioned sharply.

"A *lot*. But don't you see? This time he's made the right decision. Blackstone's attendance last night proves that. He's interested. If we can obtain even a small portion of his business for our PR firm, it'll be worth every penny Dad spent. We'd be set for life."

Jacq's lashes flickered downward, concealing her expression. How many times had she heard that line before? "Why do you suppose Blackstone wants me there?"

J.J. shrugged. "Who knows. He's just like that."

"Like what?"

"I told you. Careful. Exacting. Thorough. Unbelievably precise. That's why it's taken so long to attract his interest. He likes to examine all the possible angles before he makes a decision."

"What's so tough about making a decision?" Jacq questioned in genuine confusion. "You just do it."

"Well, not Mathias Blackstone. Unlike normal people, once he reaches a decision, he never changes his mind."

"You're kidding. Never?"

"Never. I guess that's why he works so hard to get it right the first time."

"How very black-and-white of him." Jacq shot her sister an impish grin. "Personally, I need more elbow room. That's why I like all that colorful area in between. It offers so many intriguing possibilities."

"Not Blackstone," J.J. reiterated. "None of those colors exist for him. I don't even think they're in his vocabulary. He's the most ruthless, intimidating man I've ever met. And those eyes of his!" She shivered. "It's like looking into a sea of green ice. They freeze me solid."

No, they didn't freeze, Jacq silently corrected. They mesmerized, holding her while they searched. Searched for... Her brows drew together. Searched for... *What*? Why *had* he been looking at her so intently at the party? "I'd still like to know why I have to be there," she murmured. "I'm not a Limelighter."

"You were."

A wintry coldness settled into Jacq's tone. "Briefly. Since I'm not with the firm any longer, why insist I attend this meeting? I have no influence over how you three conduct business."

"Do you plan to hold that incident against Dad for ever?" J.J. questioned in distress. "It was horrible, I admit. But it worked out in the end, right? After all, you received Grandmother's inheritance. That went a long way toward compensating you for that fiasco, didn't it?"

Jacq fought for patience. "Grandmother Lacey gave me the cottage and exactly one thousand dollars."

"So you've said. But if that's true…" J.J. frowned. "Where does your money come from? You never leave the cottage to go to work, and yet—"

Jacq averted her gaze. Her secret identity was becoming more and more difficult to keep hidden from her family. Unfortunately if they ever found out, she'd lose the precious anonymity she'd enjoyed these past few years. "The rest of you received the main house. It was a fair division," Jacq finished with careful deliberation. Thankfully, the reminder succeeded in deflecting her sister's attention.

"We get to keep the main house only as long as we don't invade your privacy." A reluctant smile quivered at the edges of her mouth. "I can't even knock on your door without fear of violating the will."

"You can knock," Jacq replied mildly. "You just can't come in without an invitation."

"Look— Could we get back to the point of this conversation? Will you come tonight?"

"I'm thinking."

"Could you think a little faster? You're not

Blackstone. Give me a simple yes or no answer. We need time to invent an excuse if you refuse.''

Jacq sighed. Her choices were clear. Since her family wouldn't dare risk encroaching on her privacy, she could refuse their request and stay home without worrying about a herd of Randells descending on her door. Grandmother's will had seen to that. Or she could attend this little meeting her father had arranged and suffer through whatever unpleasant surprises he intended to spring. There was one distinct advantage to that plan of action.

If she went, she'd have another opportunity to study Mathias Blackstone. Only this time it would be up close and personal. She could analyze his various expressions, watch him move, pin down the exact shade of those odd green eyes. Getting better acquainted with Blackstone would breathe life into her still-sleeping dragon. The temptation proved too great to resist.

"Okay, I'll do it," she said. "What time?"

"Si— Er, five-thirty. And for heaven's sake, don't be late!" J.J. made a dismissive gesture. "Although why I bother to tell you that, I don't know. It's like asking the sun not to shine."

"It is rather pointless," Jacq conceded. "But if it makes you feel any better, it isn't deliberate. Honest. I just lose track of time."

"I don't know how that's possible," J.J. grumbled. "It's not like you have anything else to occupy your thoughts. All you do is hide out in that cottage of yours and paint." A glint of curiosity shone in her dark eyes. "At least, I assume you're painting. Not that you've ever bothered to show us the results."

"Trust me. You wouldn't be interested," Jacq replied

with careful nonchalance. "Now if you'll excuse me, I'm going to hide out in my cottage some more."

"At least leave the phones plugged in so we can reach you," J.J. called. "Please?"

Jacq lifted a hand in acknowledgment as she left. Cutting through the sprawling garden at the back of the house, she headed toward the small cottage tucked at the far end of the property. Surrounded by a huge ivy-covered wall, it perched on the edge of Lake Washington. She adored her hideaway and thanked Grandmother Lacey every day for her unexpected benevolence.

After Jacq had left Limelight, she'd been adrift, not quite sure which direction her life should take. That question had been settled with one decisive conversation with her grandmother.

"You're finally going to fulfill your dream," Grandmother Lacey had announced two short months before her death. "You're going to paint. And you're going to paint full time, not just when Turk gives you the odd moment free. It's what you've always wanted and I'm going to see to it that you have a chance to succeed."

She'd been as good as her word. She'd set up a studio for Jacq in the cottage and insisted that the story ideas and sketches that had accumulated over the years be sent out to various publishing companies. Unfortunately, she hadn't lived long enough to witness Jacq's success. It had been a devastating loss. In fact, it wasn't until the will had been read that Jacq realized the full extent of her grandmother's love. She'd been left the cottage to use as a studio. And a stipulation had been included in the will ensuring privacy while she worked toward her goal. No one could enter the cottage without permission or they'd lose the main house to charity.

A sudden gust of wind tugged at her curls, whipping them into a frenzy. Wrapping her arms around her waist, Jacq ducked her head against the frigid air. The December morning felt raw, the steely gray clouds overhead heavy with the threat of rain. Next time she'd remember to grab her rain slicker. At least, she'd try to remember. Mundane matters such as that had a tendency to slip her mind. She'd lost count of the number of occasions she'd been caught in an unanticipated downpour. And in Seattle unanticipated downpours were always anticipated.

She arrived home the same instant as the skies opened. Darting inside, she slammed the heavy oak door against the elements and breathed a sigh of relief. Angelica meowed a greeting, leaping from a nearby table to rub with feline affection against her leg.

"Hello, sweetheart. I have messages, do I?"

The cat purred an acknowledgment and Jacq glanced at her answering machine. Sure enough, the light blinked with unmistakable urgency. The first six calls were from J.J., each more pressing than the last. Fortunately, Jacq had taken it into her head to go in search of a book on broad-leaved plants. She liked to make certain the background elements in her paintings were as accurate and detailed as possible. Her appearance up at the main house had spared J.J. the hassle of coming down and pounding at the front door. The last message on the tape was from her agent, raving about the sales figures on her latest children's book.

"Hello, Jack Rabbitt. Oops! Sorry, I just remembered. You don't want me leaving your pseudonym on your answering machine." Elena sighed. "I hate these stupid contraptions. I'll bet you have the phones turned off again, don't you? Anyway... I don't know what it is about elves and fairies and trolls, but your books are flying off the shelves. Those illustrations are pure magic. Hey, I have an idea. Have you ever given any thought to painting dinosaurs? They're still popular with the buying public. Or how about dragons? Can you do dragons by any chance? Just a thought.''

"Now there's a cosmic coincidence," Jacq murmured.

"Anyway, call me. Okay? *Ciao*, babe. Talk to you soon."

Jacq grinned in satisfaction. "Pretty cool, Angel. Who'd have thought three years ago we'd make such a big splash? Bless Grandmother Lacey. If it hadn't been for her..." A momentary darkness settled on her piquant features. "She gave me back my life. Didn't she, sweetheart?"

Angelica's ears twitched and Jacq decided to take that as an agreement. Walking to the back half of the cottage with the cat at her heels, she carefully secured the door between the "public" section where she entertained the occasional visitor and the "private" area.

It was here that she became her alter ego—Jack Rabbitt—author and illustrator of some of the most popular children's books currently on the market. Three years ago the first Jack Rabbitt book had hit the stores and become an overnight sensation. Since then, her popularity had seen explosive growth. It had proved a mixed blessing. Although it provided her with the independence she so desperately craved, it also brought a notoriety she hated. So far, she'd managed to keep her identity a deep, dark secret. So far. With any luck at all, she could keep it that way for the next thirty to forty years.

Stepping into the studio, Jacq felt her tension drain away. This was the one and only place she felt truly at home. She studied her surroundings with a tiny smile. Pinned around the cavernous room were a series of sketches—every last one of them of an enormous black dragon with haunting green eyes.

"Hello, Nemesis," she whispered.

Angelica meowed plaintively, fixing the beast with a suspicious gaze.

"You're not sure about him yet, are you, sweetheart?" Jacq tilted her head to one side, contemplating her work. "Give it time. Soon, he'll be awake and breathing fire. Very soon now. And then you'll find him as attractive as I do."

At precisely six o'clock, Turk opened the massive front door to the Randell mansion. "Blackstone. I'm pleased you could make it." He offered his hand along with a hearty grin.

Mathias shook hands, lifting an eyebrow as he entered. "Did you doubt I'd come? I did arrange this meeting."

"Quite right. I just meant—" Turk cleared his throat and gestured down a long hallway. "I think you'll find the library a convenient place to discuss business. Plenty of room. We can get comfortable and answer any questions you might have about Limelight International." Taking the lead, he thrust open the first door they came to.

Mathias entered the room and glanced around. As Turk had indicated, the library had been designed for comfort while offering absolute business efficiency. An impressive array of books lined the walls while an imposing oak desk dominated one end of the room. Randell utilized the other half as a sitting area. Discreet lighting illuminated plush chairs, a couch, an extra-wide coffee table and a wet bar. The liquor cabinet stood open, glasses and bottles at the ready.

The hard sell would be accomplished there, Mathias realized with a touch of cynicism. As though to acknowledge that fact, Turk's son and youngest daughter hovered on either side of a couch, waiting for him to join them. Once seated, he'd be neatly hemmed in by Randells. His eyes narrowed in displeasure. Only one component was missing. A very small, very vital component.

Mathias turned to confront Turk. "Your entire family isn't here."

"Er, no. I expect Jacqueline will show up any moment now." Turk edged closer to the sitting area. "In the meantime, why don't we—"

"We'll wait."

With that, Mathias strolled to the bookcase and began an intent study of the contents. A whispered, distinctly agitated conversation ensued from the general direction of the sitting area. No doubt they were arguing over who would go and fetch Jacq. Before they reached their decision, a sudden flurry of activity sounded behind him. He turned in time to see Jacq breeze into the room and her family start en masse toward her. They stopped in their tracks the instant they realized how their actions might be interpreted—or misinterpreted.

"Sorry I'm late," Jacq announced casually, oblivious to the undercurrents swirling around her.

Her gaze fastened on Mathias and remained there. She studied him with the same direct intensity that he often gave his own pursuits. It filled him with an absolute certainty, an instinctive knowledge that the others in the room no longer existed for her. For this brief moment in time, he had become the center of her universe. His eyes narrowed as he assessed his reaction. As someone who worked hard to avoid attracting unnecessary attention, he'd never been the center of anyone's universe. To his utter amazement, he discovered that he relished the feeling—relished it far more than wisdom dictated.

"We haven't been introduced," he stated.

A delicious smile tilted her mouth. "No, we haven't." She'd piled her wealth of curls on top of her head instead of confining them at the nape of her neck. As she approached, a multitude of escaped ringlets bounced in joyous abandonment about her slender neck and angled cheekbones. She held out her hand, saying simply, "I'm Jacq."

He captured her hand in his. "Mathias Blackstone."

She had strange eyes, the color quite unusual. One moment the irises appeared sharply brown and gold before exploding with brilliant green and gray highlights. It was as though her every thought had its own unique color combination. Fascinating. Quite fascinating.

"Okay. I'm here," she announced. "Just out of curiosity... Would you care to tell me *why* you asked me to come?"

He stilled, wondering if his expression revealed his surprise at the directness of her question. Damn. He hoped not. "I wanted to meet you," he answered just as directly.

"Why?"

"Jacq, for crying out loud," Turk interrupted with a groan. "Could we at least sit down and have a drink before you start in on the man."

"But—"

"You'll have to excuse my daughter, Blackstone." He dropped a restraining hand on Jacq's shoulder. For all their slender elegance, his fingers threatened to crush the fragile bones trapped within his grasp. "She's not renowned for her tact."

For the first time in more years than he cared to remember, Mathias acted without thinking. He snatched Jacq from her father's hold and into his own sphere of influence. "Excuse us for just a minute. I'd like to speak with your daughter," he said, his voice taking on an unmistakable edge. When Turk continued to stand there, Mathias added pointedly, "Alone, if you don't mind."

"I didn't realize— I didn't mean—" With a muttered excuse, Turk crossed to the sitting area, exchanging confused glances with Cord and J.J.

"Are you all right?" Mathias asked in an undertone, brushing a gentle hand across her shoulder.

"Dad didn't mean anything by it," Jacq replied just as quietly, fixing him with a speculative look.

He understood that look. It asked why he'd interfered, why he'd reacted like a protective lover, instead of the stranger he happened to be. And the only response he could come up with was...damned if he knew. "Your father doesn't know his own strength."

She shook her head. "He'd never deliberately harm me. But he's under pressure tonight. And when that happens he sometimes forgets that I'm not built along the same proportions as Cord or J.J."

"It's time he remembered."

Inquisitiveness gave her eyes a misty gray tint. "Is that why you're here? To remind him?"

"No." He relaxed his guard enough to smile. "Would you believe I came to meet you?"

"Me?" She shook her head, laughing softly. It was a husky, full-bodied laugh, and as with everything else about her, it held irresistible appeal. "I find that hard to believe. Although as a line, it has definite potential."

"I'll work on it." He had himself back under control—a very tenuous control, true. But it should be enough to get him through this meeting. "Shall we join the others?"

She peeked around him toward the sitting area. "They are looking rather frayed around the edges," she murmured. "I hope you're planning to put them out of their misery."

"I'll be quick. I promise."

He walked with her to the couch, blocking access to the chair the Randells had left vacant for Jacq. "Shall we get started?" Mathias said. "I have a dinner engagement at seven."

"Have a seat, Blackstone," Turk said with forced heartiness. "What can I get you to drink?"

"Nothing, thanks. I won't be staying."

J.J. stirred. "Mr. Blackstone, perhaps you'd tell us why you arranged this meeting. Are you interested in utilizing Limelight's services?"

Mathias hesitated for a fraction of a second. Until this morning, he'd have been lying if he said he had someone in need of a PR firm. Fortunately, he'd been approached just today by a man who fit the bill. He'd most likely have turned the request down, too, if it hadn't provided him with the perfect excuse to approach Limelight. "I'm interested in giving Limelight a trial run," he announced.

"We're listening," Turk said, all business.

"I have a client who's starting up an investment company and needs the sort of creative publicity only a top-notch PR firm can provide. Fair warning, he's a rather particular client."

"Particular as in difficult?" Cord asked with his father's frankness.

"Let's just say he requires special attention," Mathias replied, not in the least offended by Cord's candor. "If you're successful, I'll know your firm has the skill to handle my other business requirements." He lifted an eyebrow. "Arc you interested?"

"We're interested," Turk responded. "When do we get started?"

"I'll fax you the details first thing in the morning." He spared a quick glance at his watch. "And now if you'll excuse me, I have to go. Jacq, I'd appreciate it if you'd see me out."

He could see the protest dawning in Turk's expression. Before it could find voice, Mathias snagged Jacq's elbow and walked to the door.

"We're leaving?" she asked, amused.

"We're leaving."

She didn't say anything until they reached the front door. He found that intriguing. Most women would have demanded an explanation. But not this one. Instead, she walked beside him, her gait light and easy, her expression curious yet patient. She glanced up at him and smiled. It was an open, appealing smile, filled with an electrifying vitality.

How the hell had Turk Randell fathered such a changeling? he couldn't help but wonder.

At the front door, she hesitated. "Considering what I know of your personality—which I confess isn't all that much—I have to assume you had a reason for asking me to show you out."

"Yes."

She tilted her head to one side. "Care to clue me in?"

"Would you have dinner with me?"

She blinked in astonishment. "Dinner."

"That's the meal you consume at the end of the day," he explained gravely. "Sometimes two people will share the meal. Are you familiar with the custom?"

Humor flickered within her gaze. "Somewhat. When did you have in mind?"

"Now."

"But you told my father—" Comprehension dawned and she laughed. "Sorry to be so slow. You caught me off guard."

It would be easy to get used to the sound of that laugh, he decided. All too easy. "You haven't answered my question. Will you join me for dinner?"

She took a moment to consider, studying him with a disconcerting intensity. "Is this a business dinner or personal?"

"I imagine it could go either way," he answered honestly. "Which would you prefer?"

"I'm not sure." A new array of colors sparkled within her eyes, shades Mathias had begun to associate with the more mischievous aspects of her personality. As though to confirm his suspicion, she pulled open the door and caught his arm in hers. "Why don't we find out?"

"Well I'll be a son of a—" Turk allowed the heavy drape to fall closed. "Seems you were right, J.J."

She smiled dispassionately. "Of course I was right."

"Walked off with the girl like he owned her." Turk's brows drew together as he analyzed the possible ramifications. "So now we know what *he* wants. But what about her? Never could figure out Jacq's thinking on anything."

"She went with him, didn't she?" Cord inserted. "She wouldn't do that unless she wanted to."

"Unfortunately, we can't count on that lasting," J.J. said. "You know Jacq."

The three fell into an unhappy silence, recognizing J.J.'s remark as an indisputable fact.

"So what now?" Cord asked.

"Now we treat Jacq the same way we would an uncooperative business associate," Turk replied grimly.

J.J.'s expression cooled. She didn't like the sound of this one little bit. "You can't be suggesting blackmail."

Her father winced. "You always were far too blunt, J.J. I prefer to think of it as...persuasion. Gentle persuasion, if possible. We find a way to convince her to go along with our plans. Explain the advantages to her."

Cord snorted. "Yeah, right. Knowing Jacq, I'm sure that'll work."

Turk acknowledged his son's sarcasm with a chilly smile. "Oh, it'll work."

"How?" J.J. demanded. "If we tell her to turn left, she'll choose every direction except left. She's totally unpredictable. She doesn't even do the opposite of what we ask. She just does something different."

"There's no point in trying to second guess her," Turk agreed. "There's only one way to deal with Jacq."

"Which is?" J.J. asked apprehensively.

"We find the right angle."

"What do you mean, 'the right angle'?"

Annoyance flashed in Turk's dark eyes. "Don't be obtuse. You know what I mean. Everyone has a weakness. We just need to find Jacq's."

"Then you are talking about blackmail."

"Fine," Turk snapped, slamming his fist on the liquor cabinet. The bottles and glasses clattered discordantly.

"I'm talking about blackmail. I'm talking about finding out what she's been up to for the past three and a half years. Cord, you do the background check."

"No problem."

"J.J., I want to know her strengths and weaknesses, particularly her weaknesses. Her vulnerabilities. I want anything we can use to make her see the advantages of continuing a relationship with Blackstone."

"Dad—"

"I don't want to hear it," Turk interrupted coldly. "I don't like forcing her hand any better than you. But we don't have a choice. Do I have to remind you how much is at stake?"

"No, but—"

Turk cut her off again. "You're worrying about nothing. Jacq wouldn't have gone with Blackstone if she wasn't interested. All I'm asking is she stay interested long enough for us to strike a deal with the man." His tone turned aggrieved. "Is that so much to ask?"

"For some." J.J. turned away, wrapping her arms around her waist. "For some, it's asking the impossible."

CHAPTER TWO

"So, WHERE are we going?" Jacq asked as they walked out the front door.

"To the home of an acquaintance." Mathias hesitated on the doorstep. "It's not far from here, but you might want to bring a coat."

She shook her head, not in the least concerned. It wasn't her coat she'd miss, but her satchel of paints. She rarely went anywhere without them, though it looked like tonight she'd be forced to make an exception. "I'd have to go back to my place to get my coat and I don't feel like taking the time," she said. Nor did she feel like running the risk of being bushwhacked by Limelighters.

"Your place? You don't live...?" He indicated the house behind them with a jerk of his head.

"No. I live in a little cottage at the far end of the property right on the lake. It used to be a garage. Then it was the caretaker's quarters." Satisfaction edged her voice. "Now it's mine."

"No purse. No coat." A hint of a frown touched his brow. "I didn't mean to rush you. I can wait while you get them."

"My sweater is wool, so I should be warm enough. I'll ask if I need anything else." She dismissed the mundane subject with an easy shrug and turned to one of far greater importance. "So, don't keep me in suspense. Who are these friends? Where do they live?"

He slanted her an amused glance as they followed a

sidewalk that wove an erratic path to the driveway. "You mean, what are they serving for dinner?"

She grinned, unabashed. "Did you hear my stomach growling? I'm starving! I can't remember when I last ate." She tilted her head to one side, considering. "Not only don't I remember when, I can't even remember what the meal consisted of."

"The when, I suspect, was Turk's reception last night. As to the what... You had half a dozen shrimp, crab dip and crackers, cheese and a handful of those little round green things. I won't mention the relish tray you nabbed on your way out."

She stared in astonishment. "How in the world do you know all that?"

"I'm observant."

"Now there's an understatement," she muttered. *He'd been watching her*! While she'd been watching her relatives watch him, he'd been... Her sense of the ridiculous caught up with her and she gave a light laugh. "I guess it would have been more socially acceptable to nibble." Her voice turned wistful. "But I was awfully hungry."

"Don't they feed you?"

"I'm supposed to be able to feed myself."

"But you get preoccupied and forget." It wasn't a question.

"How did you—" She held up her hands. "Never mind. I don't want to know. Some questions are best left unanswered and I suspect this is one of them."

"It's no great mystery. I put together a few facts based on observation and came up with—"

"An inspired guess?"

"An educated supposition," he corrected gently. "I don't guess."

"That's what J.J. said," Jacq admitted. "But I thought maybe she was exaggerating."

"Not in this case."

"Oh. Well. Never mind. I won't hold it against you." She smiled brightly. "About tonight..."

He took both her comment and the change in subject in stride. "I never did answer your questions, did I? You wanted to know about my friends. I've been invited to a small dinner party and hoped you'd accompany me."

"I see." Understanding dawned, taking the edge off her enthusiasm. "You need a date."

He stopped in the middle of the walkway and removed his coat. "I don't *need* a date," he informed her, draping the heavy black wool about her shoulders. He gathered the edges of the collar beneath her chin and waited until her gaze flickered reluctantly upward to meet his. "I invited you because I wanted to."

She was instantly captivated by his translucent green eyes. They were like flaming ice, came the bewildered realization, possessing the uncanny ability to freeze and scorch at the same time. She'd never seen anything like it before. "Why?" she couldn't help asking, snuggling into the folds of his jacket. It was deliciously soft, enfolding her in unrelenting masculine warmth. "Why did you invite me?"

"Because you're different from the rest of your family. And that difference intrigues me." He released her with notable reluctance and gestured toward the black Jaguar parked at the top of the circular driveway. It crouched beneath the protective embrace of an immense oak, looking sleek and fast and decidedly lethal. "Will you come with me?"

The words were innocuous enough. And yet she felt the dragon in him stirring, awakening before her very eyes. The change captivated her, her curiosity becoming an irresistible impetus. She could either enter the predator's domain or run for the safety of her snug little cottage. The choice was hers.

There was no point in pretending which she'd select. "Okay." He smiled at her response—a smile of genuine pleasure—and Jacq had the inexplicable impression that it had been a long time since he'd allowed himself that particular luxury. "I'll come."

"I'm glad," he replied.

His Jag gave a little chirp of welcome as he deactivated the alarm system and she halted beside the car, shaking her head. "I should have known. I really should have."

He lifted an eyebrow. "Excuse me?"

"I just realized. Your car. Your clothes. Everything's black."

He opened the passenger door. "It's a comfortable color for me."

Interesting. It would appear that this particular dragon preferred life in the shadows rather than basking in the sunshine. For some reason the knowledge saddened her. "I'll have to see what I can do about that," she informed him as she lowered herself into the low-slung seat.

"Don't bother. I'm satisfied with my life as it is."

Shutting the door to punctuate his comment, he circled the car and climbed in. With a quick flick of his wrist, he turned the key in the ignition. The Jag awoke with a throaty roar, before relaxing into a steady purr. Jacq studied Mathias in silence as they zipped down the driveway. He maneuvered the car with exquisite precision, every movement graceful and specific and economical. As usual, J.J.'s assessment of the man had been right on target. He was a creature whose world consisted of only black and white, who saw life in uncompromis-ing terms of absolutes.

Up or down. Right or left. Yes or no. No exception to the rules.

"What are you thinking?" he asked unexpectedly.

Jacq decided to give him an honest, if blunt, response. "I'm thinking that I'm glad I'm me. I like my world to have colors in it."

She'd caught him off guard. "You think because I prefer black that my world lacks color?" he asked after a moment's consideration.

"Yes." She touched his arm, surprised when the mus-cles bunched beneath her fingers. "Oh, it's not just the fact that you like black. Black is an excellent color. I'm quite fond of it, myself." Especially for unruly dragons, she added the silent addendum.

"I'm relieved to hear it."

"But I'm afraid it suggests a certain rigidness of char-acter."

"Rigid." His eyes narrowed and she began to wonder if she'd been a little too blunt. "And you prefer someone who's more... What?"

"Someone who's more spontaneous," she readily ad-mitted.

"Inviting you out to dinner wasn't spontaneous enough for you?" he asked dryly.

"Ah, but was it? A spur-of-the-moment decision, I mean."

His frown deepened. "It was last night when I thought of it."

She regarded him in surprise. "You decided to invite me out then?"

"Yes."

Another possibility occurred to her. "Is that why you

arranged the meeting tonight with Turk? Why you insisted that the entire family be there?''

"Yes," he said again.

She couldn't quite believe it. "You did all that just so you could ask me out?" she demanded in astonishment.

"Sorry," he offered in a suspiciously humble voice. "Considering my limited imagination, it was the best I could come up with on such short notice."

She decided to take his comments seriously. "That's okay. It was a sweet gesture. But now there's a problem."

"Somehow, that doesn't surprise me. What sort of problem?"

"My father expects to do business with you. You can't very well tell him that the whole point of tonight's meeting was so you could ask me out."

His gaze flickered briefly in her direction before returning to the winding road ahead. "Will it offend you if I admit that the meeting this evening gave me an opportunity to address two separate issues? One business and the other personal. This investment company I mentioned needs a PR firm to help launch them in the community. If I put your father's firm together with King Investments, it will give Limelight a chance to prove themselves to my satisfaction while affording King the publicity they need to get off the ground."

She sighed, vaguely disappointed. "I see. You were killing two birds with one stone."

He hit third gear with less than his normal precision. "That's not quite how I'd have phrased it, but yes. The arrangements I made with Turk last night allowed me to have a preliminary meeting with Limelight. At the same time I could invite you out."

"An economy of effort," she said in perfect understanding. "Quite like you." She thought she heard him curse beneath his breath, but when she glanced in his direction, his expression remained blandly polite. "I don't suppose you've ever heard of a telephone?"

"Of course I have." His gaze flashed in her direction once again and she caught a fleeting glimpse of irony reflected there. "But in order to conduct a conversation, the other party has to have their phone plugged in."

Her mouth literally fell open. "How did you know that I keep it unplugged?"

"It's amazing what you can learn with a little research."

She fought off a feeling of unease. "That must be one heck of a research department you have," she muttered. Which brought up another question. "I never thought to ask J.J. what you did or why you need Limelight's help. She only mentioned that Turk's been trying to attract your attention for the last couple of years."

He lifted an eyebrow in response to that nugget of information, but didn't pursue it. "You don't know what I do for a living?" he asked instead.

"No." Jacq shrugged, feeling obligated to add, "Since I don't work for the company, I'm not up on all the pertinent details."

"But you used to work for them, didn't you?"

Her mouth compressed. "Briefly." She heard the clipped quality enter her voice, but couldn't help it. "Very briefly."

"What was your specialty?"

She shook her head, refusing to answer. "My turn. You still haven't said what you do for a living."

He turned into a narrow driveway that opened onto a sprawling estate. A dozen or so expensive foreign cars were parked close to the pillared front porch. Mathias found an open spot beneath a huge apple tree and pulled in, shutting off the engine.

"Well?" Jacq prompted impatiently. "Are you going to tell me or is it a deep, dark secret?"

"No secret. I'm a... I guess you could call me a procurer."

Releasing her seat belt, she swiveled to face him, staring in disbelief. "A *procurer*? Like a... A... You're kidding, right?"

"Nope. I'm dead serious."

She regarded him suspiciously. It couldn't be what she was thinking. Not her dragon. He wouldn't do anything so unethical. "Okay... Would you care to tell me what, precisely, you procure? Or is that a question you'd prefer I not ask?"

He relaxed into the leather seat, clearly at home in the darkness. "You have the most revealing eyes of anyone I've ever met," he commented reflectively. "You think I'm a white slaver or an international jewel thief, don't you?"

She squirmed beneath his unblinking gaze. "If it makes you feel any better, I almost immediately realized that you wouldn't do anything so awful," she confessed.

"You realized that, did you? After less than an hour's acquaintance you know me so well? Mind if I ask how you came to that conclusion?"

"It's because you're—"

He held up a hand, cutting her off. "Forget it. I suspect it has to do with colors again, doesn't it?"

"Well, yes. As a matter of fact, it does. I suspect your ethics are as well-defined as everything else in your life." She hoped he'd find the word "well-defined" a tactful alternative to "rigid." "But you did have me going for a minute there. The term 'procurer' does have a suggestive ring to it.''

''It's a fanciful word for a mundane job,'' he admitted with a smile. ''I suppose I like it because it evokes a much more interesting response than when I say I'm a middleman.''

''A middleman, huh? And what is it you're in the middle of, exactly?''

''I don't have a specialty. People come to me because they're having difficulty obtaining something they want or need. I get it for them. It's as simple as that.''

''Somehow I doubt it is.''

''It can be a challenge at times,'' was all he'd concede.

''But you've never failed to meet that challenge, have you?'' she guessed shrewdly. ''You've always succeeded in your various procurements.''

He hesitated before responding. ''Since I started the business, I've never failed.''

Something in the way he phrased his response gave her pause. But she was too interested in learning more to dwell on it. ''What sort of things do you procure?''

''Anything a person desires, so long as it's legal and ethical.''

''And who determines whether or not it's ethical?''

''I do.''

''Ah. That black-and-white quality of yours.'' A sudden thought occurred to her and she frowned. ''And Limelight International? I can't quite see you pursuing the sort of media attention Turk specializes in. How do they fit into the picture?''

''Sometimes there's no alternative.''

''In which case Limelight is a necessary evil?'' she

inquired delicately. "If there's no other way to get what you want, you'd use Turk's services?"

His smile flashed in the darkness. "I have the occasional need for a public relations firm, either for a client or for my own personal use. Since I have a large client base, it could mean a lot of business for your family."

"You have regular customers?" She found that surprising. "I wouldn't have thought yours a profession that would get repeat business."

"There are quite a few corporations I assist on a regular business. Either they're looking for a specific type of person to employ, or they're after a product or service that's not readily available."

She thought about it for a moment. Thought about all the possibilities for a man with Mathias's abilities. She'd been woefully shortsighted. There had to be a thousand different people with a thousand different requests who would pay a fortune to obtain that one item they lacked. She gazed at him with new understanding. "You have to turn away business, don't you?"

"Yes," he said simply.

"And tonight? Let me guess... You're here to make a procurement, right?"

He stiffened and she realized she'd made a lucky hit based on wild speculation. "Very clever, Jacq."

She lowered her gaze in the hopes of concealing her disillusionment. "So who or what are you procuring?"

He leaned closer, snagging one of the curls brushing her temple. It wrapped around his finger with all the determination of a fast-growing vine. "Let's set the record straight, shall we? First, I invited you out tonight because I wanted to. It had nothing to do with Limelight. Nor did it have anything to do with this evening's procurement. And second, I'm obligated to attend this party.

I brought you along because it would make the occasion more enjoyable. Selfish, but true.''

"Still... You're killing two birds with one stone again.''

He sighed. "I can see that's a practice you don't appreciate. I'll make sure it doesn't happen again.''

"Don't worry about it.''

"Polite reply, though painfully stilted.'' He waited a beat, then asked, "What's wrong, Jacq?''

She took a deep breath. "I don't like mixing work and pleasure.'' She shot him a cool, direct look. "In particular, I dislike mixing Limelight business with a personal relationship. If you're using me to get information about my family, I'd rather you be frank about it. I'll tell you what you want to know, since they have nothing to hide. But don't lie to me about what you're after.''

"Fair enough.'' He shifted closer, his eyes like flaming chips of green ice. "The truth is this... I don't give a damn about Limelight International. Any PR firm can handle the sort of business I plan to send their way, so long as they're ethical. Approaching Turk was the easiest way to get at you. Is that frank enough?''

It took a full minute to realize she was holding her breath. She released it on a ragged sigh. "Yes. That's frank enough for me.''

"I could have had Turk come to my office. But since you don't work for him, I would have lost the opportunity to obtain an introduction.''

"There were other ways to arrange a meeting,'' she reminded him.

"Such as phoning. We've already discussed why that wouldn't have worked.'' His thumb brushed the arch of her cheek, eliciting a helpless shiver. "This was the way

that occurred to me, so it's the one I chose. Still frank
enough?''

''Absolutely.'' If anything, he'd become too frank. As
much as she wanted to pull away and end the conversation, the curl he'd snagged held her anchored to within
inches of him.

''And finally, I didn't invite you tonight because I
needed a date. Nor did I invite you because you'd provide a convenient 'cover' to hide my activities. If anything you're going to be one hell of a distraction. I invited you because I was too damned impatient to wait
for a more convenient time. I wanted to get to know you
right away.''

''J.J. says you never act without examining all the
angles first,'' she protested helplessly.

His gaze took fire. ''I *have* examined all the angles.
Every last one of them. And now I'm acting.''

''*Why*?'' Bewilderment clouded her eyes. ''Why
me?''

''It's real simple, sweetheart. From the minute I saw
you I wanted you. I've never experienced such an im-
mediate attraction before. So instead of taking it slow,
finding a more traditional means of approach, I came
after you as hard and fast as I could.''

It was too much, too soon. She scrambled for a way
to change the subject. ''Tell me what you're hoping to
procure tonight. Maybe I can help.''

''Now you want to help?'' He released her curl with
great care and eased back against his seat. ''A minute
ago you refused to mix business with pleasure.''

''Oh. Well, that was my business we couldn't mix.
Your business is fine with me.'' His confused expression
almost made her laugh. Confusion looked good on him,
she decided. It devastated his self-control and allowed

her a tantalizing peek at the man behind the mask. ''I mean... I don't mind helping if it doesn't have anything to do with me. So what are you after?''

He recovered his composure with amazing speed. ''I'm here to procure information about our hostess, Lynn Davenport.''

Instantly intrigued, Jacq asked, ''What sort of information do you hope to obtain?''

He hesitated. ''I'd like to get a fix on her personality. What type of woman is she? Is she content? What are her hopes, her dreams and aspirations?''

''That's expecting a lot from a simple meeting over the dinner table,'' Jacq advised him dryly. ''How do you plan to get all that out of her in one short evening of conversation?''

''That's easy. I'll talk to her until I have the facts I need.''

''You're going to sit down and grill her? That's your plan?'' She shook her head in disgust. ''How long did you say you've been doing this?''

His smile glimmered in the darkness and it gave her a surge of satisfaction. She had the distinct impression that there weren't many individuals who managed to win a smile from him. And she'd captured several already. It showed definite promise.

''You have a better idea?'' he questioned idly.

''Maybe. Just how spontaneous are you, Mathias Blackstone?''

''Ah... A challenge. I never could resist a challenge.''

''That's good to know. But you still haven't answered my question.''

''Why don't you try me and see how spontaneous I am.''

"I was hoping you'd say that." She offered a mischievous grin. "Do the Davenports know you well?"

He shook his head. "I helped her husband with a minor transaction last month. I suppose this invitation is his way of saying thank-you."

"Interesting coincidence that his wife is now the object of a procurement."

"It isn't a coincidence."

She blinked. "You... You helped Mr. Davenport in order to get at his wife?"

"Not to get at her," he corrected calmly. "It was so I could get to know her. And yes, I helped Mel obtain something he's wanted for a long time. A fair exchange, in my opinion. Now, if everything goes well, I'll do the same for my client, and possibly for Lynn Davenport, as well."

"This information you need... It won't hurt her, will it?" Jacq asked uneasily. "I mean, this *is* for a good cause, right?"

"It's for a very good cause."

She took a split second to decide. There was a gentle reassurance in his tone and a steadiness in his gaze that helped persuade her. Whatever this procurement involved, he'd make sure it didn't harm anyone. She gave a determined nod. "In that case, let's go have some fun." She opened the car door, calling over her shoulder, "Follow my lead. Okay?"

He almost laughed aloud and it was in that precise moment that Mathias realized he didn't want Jacq Randell for his client. He wanted her for himself. He wanted her with an intensity he'd never experienced with another woman, not even his former wife.

She paused in the middle of the walkway. "Are you coming?"

Curious to see what she intended, Mathias climbed from the car and followed. She still wore his jacket. In fact, it swamped her slender figure. Her brightly patterned skirt billowing out from underneath, flicking at him like a beckoning hand. She walked toward the front door with a purposeful step. He liked that, liked even more the way her brown and gold streaked curls bounced in rhythm with her stride.

One of these days he'd free those curls so they could spill across her creamy shoulders to the tender slopes of her breasts as nature intended. Then he'd lower her onto his bed and watch her hair tumble in glorious abandonment across the sheets. And finally he'd sink his fingers deep into those soft, vibrant curls at the same moment he sank himself deep into her soft, vibrant feminine warmth.

There was only one stumbling block. He suspected Jacq would prove a difficult woman to woo to bed. Her eyes reflected an intense wariness. She'd been burned at some point. Badly. And of course, there was that other matter to resolve. Once he'd proven to his satisfaction that Jacq Randell and Jack Rabbitt were one and the same, he'd have to deal with the problems that would create. But he'd find a way. Until then, he'd have to exercise both patience and delicacy.

Without a doubt, it would take a full measure of both to procure this particular woman.

CHAPTER THREE

THE minute Jacq stepped foot inside the Davenports', she knew she'd found a friend. Walking into Lynn Davenport's home was like viewing the woman's heart and soul. Jacq's first impression of the house was of elegance and warmth accented with a subtle blend of delicate colors. Next she noticed the natural-fibered rugs and furniture. Christmas decorations had made their appearance already, overrunning the place and proclaiming to the world that the Davenports thoroughly enjoyed the season. And even though it was December, fresh cut flowers filled a nearby vase.

Lynn had done the arrangement herself, Jacq would have bet on it. The blossoms hadn't been chosen to fit the decor, but rather because they were favored flowers. There was an artless grace to the display, an eclectic blending of colors and scents.

No question. Mathias had found himself a winner with this couple.

Mel Davenport, a large, gruff man at least ten years older than his late-thirties wife, introduced himself. "Mathias said he might bring a guest. Glad to have you join us."

Jacq held out her hand. "I'm Jacq Randell. You really don't mind that I tagged along? You see..." She beamed. "We just got engaged today."

Beside her, Mathias choked.

"Congratulations, you old son of a gun," Mel said, thudding Mathias on the back. "You sure are a deep one. Never gave a hint you were on the verge of marriage.''

"It was very sudden," Mathias replied in a masterpiece of understatement.

"Well, it's a lovely surprise," Lynn responded with a warm smile.

Jacq peeked up at Mathias. "But a pleasant surprise, right, sweetheart?''

He wrapped an arm around her and growled into her ear, "I'll show you how pleasant later tonight, darling.''

Lynn laughed at the byplay. "Mathias Blackstone, you're every bit as wicked as Mel. He's a tease, too.''

Jacq snuggled against Mathias, amazed that she felt secure enough to do so. This man had the oddest effect on her. "Just look at how they've decorated," she said, changing the subject to one of far greater importance. "They have colors.''

Mathias sighed.

"You've done a wonderful job," Jacq chattered on to their hostess. "I'm serious. It's quite beautiful.''

"Thank—"

"You didn't use a professional decorator, did you?"

"Jacq—" Mathias muttered in warning.

She slanted him a puzzled look. "Was I being rude? I meant it as a compliment. The colors, the furnishings, the flowers. Even the balance and flow of the room. It isn't just a setting. Haven't you realized?'' She gave him a sharp elbow to the ribs so he'd pay attention. Men could be so obtuse at times. The full spectrum of Lynn Davenport's personality was on display and he hadn't even noticed! "Mathias, this house is an extension of a real, live person. To put it simply, it's Lynn.''

Mel Davenport spoke up. "You're quite right. Lynn decorated the place without a lick of outside advice.''

He wrapped a loving arm around his wife. "Even when I'm alone in the house, her presence is all around me. It's a wonderful feeling."

Lynn positively glowed at the praise, the glance she shared with her husband sizzling the air. "I had no idea you thought that."

"Well, now you do. So don't you dare change a thing."

"I wouldn't dream of it. Not after such an effusive compliment."

Davenport turned his attention to Mathias. "I like your fiancée, Blackstone," he said. "She's a sharp cookie."

"Very sharp," Mathias agreed dryly, rubbing his bruised ribs. "She certainly keeps me jumping."

Davenport chuckled. "Now that I believe. Come on in and let me introduce you two around."

Jacq soon discovered that the Davenports' friends were an eclectic bunch and she found the next several hours a sheer delight. The major disadvantage with her current profession was how little time it afforded her to interact with others. She'd turned into a hermit, she realized in disgust. She'd allowed the unfortunate events of four years ago to change her view of the world and the people in it.

Well, tonight she'd escape her self-imposed prison and enjoy herself. By helping Mathias, perhaps she could help herself.

Perhaps she could learn to trust again.

"I'm starving!" Jacq announced with such undisguised enthusiasm that everyone at the table laughed in appreciation.

Mathias leaned back in his chair, content to simply

observe his "fiancée" in action. The Davenports and their guests had been kept amused all night—either by Jacq or by her outrageous stories or in response to one of her rapid-fire comebacks. Tonight had certainly been a revelation.

He wasn't quite sure what he'd expected—perhaps a more feminine version of Turk's bulldog nature. Instead he'd discovered an open, vibrant, exciting woman who took exquisite delight in the ridiculous. What she didn't realize was where her sense of the ridiculous would land her.

So they were engaged now, were they? He lifted his wineglass and studied her over the rim. Her impetuous announcement had not only sealed her fate, but would bring about an interesting—if inevitable—conclusion to her little game. Only one aspect of the entire situation surprised him—the conclusion he had in mind would occur far sooner than he'd envisioned.

He'd first become attracted to Jacq during his weeks of research. All the bits and pieces of information he'd gathered had added up to a very intriguing whole. The more he'd learned, the more he'd anticipated their eventual meeting. And then he'd attended the Limelight reception. From the moment he'd set eyes on Jacq, he'd known their paths were destined to merge. They'd just hit that juncture months ahead of schedule.

So much for meticulous planning.

He'd always thought he'd take his time weighing the pros and cons before taking another wife. After all, it was his nature to carefully analyze each move before acting. But with Jacq... He buried his smile in his wineglass. He'd simply known. Even with all the darkness shadowing his heart and soul, he'd still known. He'd taken one look at her and realized she was the only woman in the world capable of returning color to his bleak world.

"My goodness," Lynn said unexpectedly. "You're not wearing an engagement ring, Jacq. You didn't lose it, did you?"

Mathias glanced at his adorable bride-to-be, curious to see how she'd handle this one. Not that he need have worried.

"Oh, it didn't fit," she said blithely. "Mathias has to have it sized so it doesn't fall off in my soup."

"What a shame," Lynn sympathized. "I'd love to have seen it. Is it a diamond?"

Jacq peeked over at Mathias, her eyes bright with mischief. "It's not a traditional sort of ring at all. It's very unusual."

"For you, my dear, it would have to be," Mel said, lifting his glass in a salute.

"Don't keep us in suspense," another guest exclaimed. "Tell us what it looks like."

"It's a gold band fashioned into a dragon," Jacq said with an odd little smile. "And the tail wraps around my finger all the way to the knuckle."

"A dragon? That is unusual," Lynn commented. "I assume you collect them?"

"Oh, yes." Jacq's gaze fastened on Mathias. "It's a recent obsession. And this one is a particularly stunning piece of artwork. You see, he's clutching a heart-shaped ruby in his claws. And the eyes! They're the finest pair of emeralds I've ever seen."

"It sounds gorgeous." Lynn turned impulsively to Mathias. "You'll have to get it sized as soon as possible so Jacq can show it off the next time you come."

"I'll do my best," he replied. "But I rather the jeweler not rush. I wouldn't want him to botch the job because he's in too much of a hurry.''

"Oh, dear," Jacq piped up. "In that case, maybe you shouldn't bother having it sized. I wouldn't want it ruined. I could just wear the ring the way it is." She waggled the fingers of her left hand at him, laughter rippling through her voice. "Why don't I go ahead and try?"

"That's what you said when I first gave you the ring," he retorted blandly. "You didn't allow me a minute's peace until I gave in. Do I need to remind you what happened then?"

Jacq cupped her chin in her hand. "Oh, yes, please! Tell me what happened."

Mel burst out laughing. "You act like you don't know."

She gave an abashed smile. "I just want Mathias to have the opportunity to rub it in."

Mathias inclined his head. "Very kind of you, my love."

"Well? Go ahead and say it," she prompted.

"Say what? I told you so?"

"It's only fair that I let him give me a hard time about it," she supplied for the benefit of their audience, "because the ring fell off, just like he'd warned."

"I have no intention of rubbing it in," he protested. "That would be far too cruel…and far too easy."

She chuckled. "True enough. You're very good to me, I'm the first to admit. That's why I'll let you tell everyone what happened after that." She looked at him, her gaze full of anticipation, eagerly waiting to see where he'd take the story next.

"We then spent a full hour searching my apartment

because I allowed sentiment to overrule common sense," he responded promptly.

She wrinkled her nose at him. "I'll bet *that* doesn't happen often."

"Only around you," he assured with complete sincerity. "If I hadn't thought to move the headboard away from the wall, I doubt we'd ever have found the damned thing."

She smiled sweetly. "That's what you get for trying to be creative. Next time don't tie me to the headboard and maybe I won't lose my ring behind the bed."

"Mmm. We could have used the ceiling hook and handcuffs, but they pinch. My wrists are still sore from our last go-round."

Jacq dismissed his comment with a wave of her hand. "That's just because you left them on too long. If you hadn't misplaced the key—"

"*I* didn't misplace it!"

"—it wouldn't have been nearly so painful." She heaved an exaggerated sigh. "Not that I'd want to go through all that again. I don't know why you couldn't have called a locksmith instead of bothering the police with our little predicament."

Mathias struggled to look suitably contrite. "Sorry, darling. My big toe couldn't manage more than 9-1-1."

Lynn stared from one to the other, openmouthed. Then she began to giggle. "Oh, you two! You're pulling our legs, aren't you?"

"Well... Maybe a little," Mathias conceded. "To be honest, we don't use handcuffs."

"Not anymore. They really do pinch," Jacq added irrepressibly.

"Have you set a date, yet?" Mel demanded once the laughter had died.

"Mathias insists on next Thursday," Jacq said, helping herself to another roll.

Mathias smiled in appreciation. Damn, she was quick. With one crazy conversation, she'd painted a fantasy life he craved to turn into reality. "*You* said Thursday, darling," he corrected. "If you'll recall, *I* said Christmas."

Her brows drew together and she paused in the middle of buttering her roll. "Not next Thursday? I could have sworn you said Thursday."

"Christmas *is* a Thursday. That's why we decided it would be more romantic if we waited until then. That way we could have the first baby by Halloween."

To his utter satisfaction, she choked on her roll.

He gave her a look of exaggerated concern. "You did say you wanted to start a family right away, didn't you?" To the table at large, he announced, "She'd like an even half dozen."

"Two," she hastened to correct.

"We'll compromise. Four."

Jacq's mouth curved upward and her hazel eyes gathered in the light, reflecting bits of sunny gold and rich brown and misty gray. "I give up. Four it is. But at least two of them have to be girls."

"Never fear. We'll just keep at it until you have your two girls." He offered a slow, teasing smile. "Even if it takes a dozen boys to get them."

Her laughter rang out, irresistible and thoroughly charming. "All right, all right. I give up. I'll take the first four I'm given. Just so long as they're happy and healthy, I don't care."

A fierce sense of possessiveness took hold, one Mathias couldn't control—one he had no desire to control. He saw an image of Jacq, large with his child, saw little girls with mops of blond-streaked curls and boys with bright hazel eyes. And though he waited, knowing the bitter consequences of chasing such an impossible dream, the darkness didn't come. With that one simple laugh, she banished the shadows, holding the terrible nightmares temporarily at bay.

There was no longer any question.

She was meant to be his.

Mathias caught hold of Jacq's hand and pulled her down beside him on the couch. To his private amusement, she nestled into his embrace as though they really were an engaged couple. Matters were progressing nicely on all fronts, he decided. But then, he'd found that careful planning usually guaranteed excellent results.

"What are you looking so smug about?" she asked suspiciously.

"I'm being thoughtful, not smug," he replied, deciding to avoid the truth at all costs and thus prevent a temporary setback to his master plan. He doubted "Miss Spontaneity" would appreciate the effort he'd expended in order to carry off this little dinner engagement. "How do you think the evening's going?"

She glanced toward the Davenports and their guests, all of whom were grouped around the painting Mathias had "procured" for Mel last month. "I like them," she replied, carefully sidestepping a direct answer. Not that he let her get away with it.

"So do I. But that isn't what I meant. What's your impression of Lynn?"

"She's wonderful. Gracious, charming, genuine."

"And..." he prompted.

"And shy. She's been hurt at some point in the past."

Mathias lifted an eyebrow. "What gives you that impression?"

"Two things. There's a certain wariness about the eyes. A bit of hesitation in the way she answers questions. And then there's Mel."

"What about him?"

"Haven't you noticed?" She shifted closer and Mathias obligingly lowered his head so she could whisper in his ear. He took full advantage of the opportunity to align her more firmly against him. Soft feminine curves calibrated precisely with hard masculine angles. The fit was sheer perfection. "See how protective he is?" she said.

"Of course he's protective. She's his woman."

"Oh, for—"

Her curls quivered in response to her exasperation, brushing the side of his face and branding him with silken fire. He gritted his teeth against the sensuous abrasion. What the hell had happened to his self-control? One touch from a pint-size sprite and it evaporated like desert dew. More than anything, he wanted to palm that stubborn little chin and kiss her senseless. It took every ounce of inner resolve to resist the temptation. This was neither the time nor the place. Although he'd better find that time and place—and soon.

"Isn't that what you meant?" he asked with remarkable calm for a man in his condition. "He's not being protective because she's his woman?"

"Yes. No!" She let out an aggrieved sigh. "For your information, I'm talking about something a little more refined than caveman etiquette."

His eyebrows winged upward. "Caveman etiquette?"

"You know what I mean." Her index finger thumped against his chest. "You, Tarzan. Me, Jane. Jane belong to Tarzan. Whack Jane on the head with a club and drag her off to the cave. Get it? Caveman etiquette."

"Um... Didn't Tarzan live in a tree?"

Her warm breath exploded against his ear, nearly taking the top of his head off. It was all he could do not to grab his enchanting fiancée by her curly topknot and make a beeline for the nearest cave. Or tree. Or bed.

"Will you be serious?" she demanded irritably.

"I am always serious," he said, perfectly serious.

"Oh, very funny." Before he could give her a personal demonstration of the level of his seriousness, she inclined her head toward the far side of the room. "Now pay attention and look at Mel. See how he's standing? And did you catch that look? It's more than a natural protectiveness. It's like she's a delicate piece of crystal that might shatter if touched."

Mathias frowned, becoming instantly focused. Damned if she wasn't right. "Was he like that earlier?"

Jacq's brows drew together. "You know..." she said slowly. "I don't think he was. I mean, he was. But not quite to this extent."

"Wonder what set him off?"

"Mathias?" She gazed up at him uneasily. "This procurement of yours. You're positive it's nothing that will harm Lynn? I like her."

"So do I, honey."

"No, I mean, I *really* like her. She's sweet and kind and nice. I haven't known a lot of people like that."

"Haven't you?" His eyes narrowed and he felt a renewed surge of caveman etiquette. Only this time, it had little to do with lust. Unless it was blood lust. "I'm real sorry to hear that. You'll have to tell me about it sometime."

"Too long and boring a story," she retorted crisply. And far too private, her expression clearly said. "Let's concentrate on Lynn. I'd feel just awful if we did something to hurt her."

We. Damn, that sounded good. Did she even realize that she'd subconsciously paired them, that she openly referred to them as a team? "We won't hurt her. That's why we're taking this approach. So we can get a feel for the situation."

"Well, you'd better be right about that. Because I'm not the only one who'll kill you if you cause her any harm." Her gaze switched to their host. "Mel will rend you limb from limb."

"Then I'll have to be careful, won't I?" he replied calmly.

Jacq bit down on her lip. "*We'll* have to be careful."

At that, Mathias allowed himself another brief smile of satisfaction.

Jacq nabbed Mathias's coat and stepped through the French doors onto the Davenports's deck. The chilly night air warned of a coming frost and she pulled the heavy wool more tightly about her. The evening was going well, she decided. Since her conversation with Mathias, she'd learned all sorts of fascinating details about both Davenports. With luck, it would help.

A small noise warned Jacq that she wasn't alone. Catching sight of a splash of pale peach at the far end of the deck, she called out, "Lynn? Is that you?"

Lynn swiveled to face her, offering a smile that seemed a bit too bright and cheery. "It was such a beautiful evening, I thought I'd look at the stars."

"If it weren't for the clouds, they'd be beautiful," Jacq concurred.

"Oh." Lynn's smile faltered. "I guess you caught me."

"Is there something wrong?" Jacq questioned gently. "Perhaps it would help to talk."

"I...I don't want to burden you."

"It wouldn't be a burden." Jacq perched on the edge of the railing. "What's up?"

Lynn gazed out at the night, a sad smile playing about her mouth. "I guess it was all the talk about family and children at dinner. It can be...painful. Especially around Christmastime."

Jacq schooled her tone to reflect only a hint of the compassion that gripped her. "You don't have any children?"

"No. We wanted them. Desperately. But Mel..." She gave a helpless shrug. "It wasn't possible. Most of the time we don't mind. We're so happy together. It's just every once in a while, it catches up with me."

"I'm sorry I added to it," Jacq said sincerely.

Lynn's head jerked up. "Please! Don't be sorry. You weren't to know."

"Is there anything I can do?"

"Would you mind talking to me for a few minutes? Just until I get myself under control. These crying jags don't happen often. But when they do, I prefer to keep them from Mel."

"And he pretends not to notice."

"He tries." Lynn wrapped her arms around her waist. "It distresses him terribly when I get upset."

Jacq thought of Mathias and nodded. "Men have this uncontrollable urge to protect their women," she said in total understanding. "I imagine Mel feels helpless when it comes to something like this. He wants to make it right and he can't. For a powerful man, that can be a frustrating position."

"My husband was right. You are astute." Lynn forced

a brave smile to her lips. "Thank you for talking to me. You've helped immensely. Could I ask for one more favor?"

"Sure."

"Would you mind keeping this conversation between the two of us? It's so personal..." She trailed off awkwardly.

Jacq hopped off the railing. "My lips are sealed. Is there another way inside? We'll need to freshen up if we don't want to look like windblown disasters."

"Smart and tactful. Two rare qualities these days. I'm glad Mathias brought you along this evening so we could meet," Lynn said impulsively.

"So am I."

This time, Lynn's smile appeared more genuine. "He's a lucky man to have you."

"I'll be sure to tell him that."

"Tell me what?"

Jacq sent a startled look toward the far side of the porch. Mathias stepped from beneath the shadowed overhang of the house and approached. She planted her hands on her hips. "All this time we've been going together and I never realized how sneaky you were," she scolded.

"It's not my fault," he responded mildly. "It's the shoes. Have I interrupted something?"

"Not at all." Jacq crossed the deck to join him. "Miss me?"

He wrapped an arm around her. "More than you know. So what were you supposed to tell me?"

"How lucky you are to have me. At least according to our hostess." She caught the assessing glance he shot Lynn and hastened to distract him. "I was just on my way to find you."

"Looks like I've saved you the effort."

"So you did." She slipped from his grasp and tugged him back the way he'd come. "We'll catch up with you later, Lynn. Okay?"

"I'll meet you indoors," their hostess agreed.

As soon as she'd moved out of earshot, Mathias asked, "What was all that about?"

Jacq gazed at him, wide-eyed. "What was all what about?"

"Don't give me the innocent routine. I'm talking about your discussion with Lynn."

"Oh, that."

"Yeah, that."

"It was just girl talk."

"Oh, really?" He threw a glance over his shoulder, watching as the topic of their conversation disappeared inside. "If that's all, then why did you hustle me away from her like I'm some sort of plague-carrier? Tell me what you talked about."

"Actually, I can't," she informed him regretfully.

His gaze shifted to clash with hers and his eyes narrowed. "Can't? Or won't?"

"Can't. Won't." She shrugged. "Same difference. The point is, I promised Lynn. She asked that I keep our conversation confidential and I told her I would. You don't really expect me to betray her trust, now do you?"

"Yes, I damned well do. You seem to forget why we're here tonight."

"I haven't forgotten a thing. And just to set the record straight, obtaining information is the reason *you're* here tonight," she corrected carefully. "I came because you invited me out to dinner."

For some reason her comment annoyed him. His jaw

tensed and it took a minute before he responded. "Jacq, this is important."

"I know it's important." She turned, her expression serious. "But what you don't realize is that what Lynn said to me is something she'd never have said to you. If you'd come alone to do your procuring, you wouldn't have gotten this information, anyway. So my not giving it to you isn't going to change a thing."

"That has to be the most convoluted piece of logic I've ever heard!" he snapped.

"Give me time!" she snapped right back. "I can get much more convoluted than that."

"I don't doubt it for a minute."

They glared at each other for an endless minute. Then Jacq sighed. "You're not going to budge on this, are you?"

"Not an inch."

"Me, neither." A tiny frown puckered her brow. "It's been such a fun evening. I'd rather not spoil it with a fight. Do you suppose we could table this discussion for another time?"

He stilled and she wondered what she'd said to cause such an interesting reaction. And then she realized. "Another time" meant another time. It suggested they'd see each other again.

Before she could backtrack, he reached out and snagged her around the waist, tucking her securely against him. "An excellent suggestion. Now why don't we go wish everyone a pleasant evening. I'm sure they'll understand if we cut out early. After all, we are newly-weds."

"Newly engaged," she corrected, then sighed. "What am I saying?"

"You're saying that we've had an interesting first date. And you're looking forward to our next one."

She pulled back slightly to look up at him. "Is there going to be a next one?"

"There's no question about it. Shall I prove it to you?"

She stared at him, intrigued. "How?"

A hot glow lit his eyes, the green growing positively incandescent. "Like this...."

CHAPTER FOUR

MATHIAS cupped the back of Jacq's head and captured her mouth in a brief, intense kiss. Clearly a single sampling wasn't sufficient, for he came back for another. This one was slower and deeper, more passionate. Jacq wrapped her arms around his neck and gave herself over to sheer sensation. How had her sister described him?

Precise. Yes, that was it. Precise. If by that J.J. meant Mathias knew exactly what to do, Jacq couldn't argue with fact. He'd figured out how to stoke a woman's desire, to submerge her ever so gently into the flames. The decisive melding of lips, that delicious tangle of tongues, the sweet tasting of new, distinctive flavors. Pure precision.

Careful. That had been another of J.J.'s descriptions, Jacq recalled hazily. And Mathias was careful, all right. No question about that. He took care in the way he held her. Tight. Protective. Careful to lock hips and thighs. Close. Suggestive. Careful to ensure that he anticipated her every desire. Swift. Exacting. But most of all he was...

Thorough. Oh, yes. He was very thorough. Thorough, knowledgeable, delicious. Rocking her closer, he caught her lower lip in his teeth and ever so slowly tugged. An unexpected tingle started at her toes and flashed upward. She jumped, utterly shocked.

"What caused that?" she asked in wonder.

His surprise matched hers. "Electricity, if I'm not

mistaken. Or maybe lightning. We were definitely hit by something.''

"You...ah..." She cleared her throat. "You ever have that happen before?"

"Never."

"Thank heavens. I thought maybe I'd been missing something all these years." She grinned, lifting her mouth to his. "So we were zapped by electricity or lightning or something? That's good. Right?"

"Yeah. Real good." He lowered his head, his mouth brushing hers. "Maybe we should try again, just to make a positive identification."

Instantly, the tingle surged through her and she made an astounding discovery. Lightning did strike twice in the same place.

Jacq worked obsessively throughout the night, painting dragon after dragon. Still, she couldn't breathe life into her creation. It was the eyes, she finally decided, throwing down her brush in disgust. Those damned eyes of his. For the life of her she couldn't get the expression right—that intriguing mix of fire and ice. Nor had she found the perfect color. She'd blended every combination of green in her inventory and still hadn't hit on the right shade.

Finally, she gave up and crawled into bed.

An hour later, a pounding at the door woke her from a sound sleep. "Go away!" she said with a moan, dragging a pillow over her head.

"I know you're in there, Jacq!" J.J.'s muffled shout came from the far side of the front door. "We need to talk!"

Wearily, Jacq dragged herself from the bed and flung

open the door, squinting against the weak sunshine filtering through the clouds. "Who died?" she demanded.

"At a guess, I'd say it was you," J.J. informed her after a pointed scrutiny. "You look like something Angelica dragged in."

"Gee, thanks. I love you, too."

J.J. tapped an impeccably shod foot against the stone doorstep. "Well? Am I allowed in or not?"

Jacq propped herself against the doorjamb and swept a hand through the air in a halfhearted welcome. "What's up?" she asked as J.J. entered the cottage.

"You tell me. What's going on between you and Blackstone?"

"That's what you woke me to ask?" Jacq closed the front door and padded to the sofa. Collapsing onto the cushions, she flung an arm across her eyes. "There's nothing going on. May I go back to bed now?"

"You went out with him last night, didn't you? How long have you known him? Why didn't you tell us you two were... Were..."

Jacq peeked out from beneath her elbow. "Yes? Were...what?"

"You know!"

"We had dinner, that's all. We aren't...you know. We've never...you know. I doubt we ever will...you know. There. Feel better now?"

J.J. perched on the edge of the closest chair and shook her head. "Actually, I don't. Dad is desperate. He needs Blackstone's business. Correction. *We* need Blackstone's business. I think he was hoping that you and Blackstone were..."

"You knowing?" Jacq offered dryly. "Well, we're not."

"There isn't any chance that you will in the near future?" J.J. questioned delicately.

Jacq's eyes narrowed. "I thought Mathias was the only one in the procurement business. Or have you Limelighters found a new profession?"

Bright color leaped to J.J.'s cheeks. "I didn't mean that." She jumped to her feet and paced the small room. "All right, maybe I did, which just proves how bad the situation is." She turned to face Jacq. "Did Blackstone give you any idea whether or not we're in?"

"If you mean, whether or not Limelight is his PR firm of choice, no. He hasn't said a word. Isn't it dependent on how well you deal with this client of his?"

"Yes." J.J.'s ice-calm composure showed severe cracks. "But Dad's hoping you'll have some influence over the man. He wants you to make nice-nice, help him see the advantages of using our firm."

"I'm not a Limelighter anymore," Jacq said as gently as she could. "Remember?"

"You could still help. Drop a hint in his ear at an opportune moment."

Jacq sat up. "Please don't put me in the middle of this."

"You're already in the middle. Jacq..." J.J. moistened her lips. "It would be simpler if you'd cooperate. Dad will do *anything*, sacrifice *anything* to get at Blackstone."

"You mean any*one*, don't you?"

Slowly J.J. nodded. "He's not thinking straight. Whatever path leads to Blackstone is the path he'll take. Don't be on that path, Jacq. You'll either get swept along or run over."

Jacq set her chin at a stubborn angle. "I've played that game once before. I won't do it again."

"You may not have any choice. At least think about it. Limelight is in a precarious position right now and it's going to get worse if Blackstone doesn't come through. We need his business."

"And I'm supposed to get it?"

"I'm sorry, Jacq." A bleak darkness settled in J.J.'s gaze. "There may be no other option. The way our financial situation is right now, we either succeed with Blackstone or we go under."

The name on the smoked-glass door was very discreet. In clean, simple lettering, "Blackstone" had been etched in black. Pushing open the door, Jacq realized that she'd entered Mathias's personal lair. She couldn't help smiling. It reflected his personality exactly.

The reception area had been decorated in black, white and gray—clean white walls, plush dove gray carpeting, couches and chairs flecked with all three colors and a flashy black desk for the receptionist/secretary. Charcoal etchings framed in black lacquer decorated the walls and two huge shiny black urns filled with white and gray silk flowers flanked the couch.

"Oh, Mathias," Jacq muttered beneath her breath. "If I do nothing else, I swear I'm going to bring some color into your life."

"May I help you?" the black-gray-and-white-garbed receptionist asked in a I-know-you-don't-have-an-appointment tone of voice.

Jacq dutifully curtailed her perusal, almost choking when she read the woman's nameplate. "Just out of curiosity, Mrs. White," she couldn't resist asking, "was the name a prerequisite for the job?"

"I beg your pardon?"

Oops. Starchy, with no sense of humor. How unfortunate. Jacq offered a conciliatory smile. "Never mind. Is Mathias available? And no, I don't have an appointment." She might as well get that out of the way straight off. "If he can't see me, I'll just leave his coat with you."

Mrs. White picked up the phone. "And your name?"

Jacq couldn't resist. She should try, but apparently she didn't have the required strength of character. Dropping her satchel of paints to the rug, she perched on the edge of the desk and said, "Oh, just tell him it's his fiancée."

"His...?" The receiver crashed against the cradle and Mrs. White shoved back her chair. "One moment please." With a surprising lack of decorum, she bustled to a large set of black double doors, thrust them open and scurried inside. The doors slammed behind her.

Settling herself more comfortably on the desk, Jacq swung her foot and counted slowly to ten. When she reached six she glanced toward the double doors. Mathias stood in the threshold, leaning against the jamb. Mrs. White hovered not far behind, looking thoroughly flustered.

"Oh, hi, sweetheart," she said with a wide, sunny smile.

His mouth twitched in response. "Hello, darling." He approached, the elegance and grace of his walk enough to put even her cat, Angelica, to shame. Holding out his hand, he helped her off the desk. "Don't you like our chairs?" he asked.

"Not really." She nabbed her satchel from off the floor. "I'm allergic to the color."

"Then try the couch next time. You've thrown poor Mrs. White quite off stride sitting on her desk like that."

She wrinkled her nose at him. "And I'll bet you thought it couldn't be done."

"It just goes to show that you're a much better troublemaker than I gave you credit for. I'll file that away for future reference."

"Don't bother," she said, breezing past him toward his inner sanctum. "You'd be smart to keep that file right where you can get your hands on it."

He chuckled and Mrs. White's mouth dropped open in sheer astonishment. "I suspect you're right. Something tells me I'm going to need it very soon." Following her into the office, he said, "Hold my calls, Ebbie."

"Certainly, Mr. Blackstone." She scurried past them, shooting Jacq a look that contained equal parts fascination and disapproval. "I'll buzz you when your two o'clock appointment arrives."

"Put her in the conference room, if you would. I'll meet with her there."

"Yes, sir."

Mathias closed the double doors and leaned against them. "This is a pleasant surprise."

Jacq crossed to the middle of the room and slowly turned around. "Good grief, Mathias! I don't think I've ever seen such thorough use of black lacquer before."

"I assume that's not a compliment."

She gave an apologetic shrug, then suddenly remembered that she still wore his coat. Slipping it off, she held it out to him. "This is my excuse for being here."

"You didn't need an excuse." He left his stance by the door and took the coat from her, tossing it across a nearby chair. "I appreciate your returning it, but I have to admit I'm puzzled."

She tilted her head to one side. "Really? About what?"

"What did you bring to wear home?"

She stared blankly at him for a long minute, then gave a reluctant laugh. "Good question. But, don't worry about it." She gave a careless shrug. "I'll make do."

"Let me guess. Your sweater is wool and will keep you warm enough."

"Something like that."

"I'd feel better if you'd take my coat when you leave." He held up a hand as she started to argue. "I insist."

She gave in with good grace. "Thanks. I appreciate it." Prowling restlessly toward his desk, she studied the surface. It was made of smoked glass, not so much as a fingerprint marring the surface. He'd centered the blotter directly in front of his chair. Files formed tidy, symmetrical stacks around the blotter. She bent over and examined the glass.

"What are you doing?"

"Just trying to see if the desktop is marked off in grids."

He gave her that bewildered look she so enjoyed. "You've lost me," he stated. "But then, I suspect that's going to be a commonplace occurrence with you."

There it was again. That hint that their relationship had a future. "Everything on your desk is so neatly organized, I just figured you must have rows and columns etched into the glass to help you keep it that way."

"No, it's a natural talent."

"Hmm. Somehow I'm not surprised. I suspected from the start that you were grid-oriented. This just proves it."

"Grid-oriented," he repeated. "An interesting concept. But I suspect that isn't what you came here to discuss. Do you want to get to it? Or would you prefer to continue dancing around the subject?"

She gave up on the desk and crossed to the black lacquer entertainment center. "I assume you're talking about Lynn," she said, glancing over her shoulder.

"Yes. I'm talking about Lynn. She gave you some personal information about herself last night, didn't she?"

"Yes, she did," Jacq admitted, seeing no point in lying. "What is this?" She picked up a heavy, vaguely octagonal object made out of some sort of coarse stone.

"I haven't a clue. It came with the decorator."

She lifted her eyebrows. "Is there anything in this office that you bought for yourself?"

"The desk, the stereo system and Mrs. White. Oh. And the cat."

That caught her attention. "A cat?" she asked in delight, returning the chunk of stone to its original position. "Where?"

He inclined his head to the corner of the room. There on a lamb's wool blanket sat a mangled marmalade tomcat. He watched warily as she approached, his raggedy ears twitching. She stooped in front of him and held out her hand. He sniffed her fingers suspiciously, then left the security of his nest and twined about her legs. A noisy rumble emitted from his throat.

"That's a first," Mathias observed. "Nemesis doesn't usually like people."

Nemesis! Jacq fought to hide her amusement. She found it an interesting coincidence. It would seem her sleeping dragon-to-be had been aptly named, after all. "So you don't like people," she murmured to the cat, giving his chin a gentle tickle. "Have they been mean to you?"

"He was one of my first procurements," Mathias explained. "My... A boy noticed the owner's abusive behavior and asked me to intervene."

"And you did," she said without question.

"I did." He folded his arms across his chest and leaned against the edge of the desk. "As fascinating as this discussion is, I don't think you came here to discuss my cat any more than you came to discuss my being grid-oriented."

"You're right," Jacq admitted, returning to the entertainment center. She wanted to look at the stereo since it was the only other item in the room—besides the desk and the cat—that Mathias had chosen. Nemesis followed, sitting attentively at her heels.

She examined the complex system. It contained a CD player with a one hundred-piece changer, a cassette deck, and a turntable—which came as a surprise. She'd assumed turntables were obsolete. There was also one piece of machinery that left her completely clueless, and what she presumed was the actual stereo. Buttons and digital readouts covered the front of each piece of equipment. Three remote controls were positioned in a neat row on top of the unit. She picked up the first.

"Uh, Jacq?"

She stared at the array of buttons on the slim black wand. Temptation beckoned. "Yes?"

"I wouldn't suggest—"

Her thumb clipped the largest and Wagner boomed from the two huge sub-woofers and four smaller speakers positioned equidistant around the room. She jumped, the remote tumbling from her hand. Nemesis streaked under the desk, his hair standing up in yellow and white tufts. With an expression of calm resignation, Mathias crossed to her side. Bending down, he picked up the remote and keyed another button.

The silence was deafening.

Jacq sighed. "Sorry, Nemesis." To Mathias, she said, "Don't touch, right?"

Amusement glimmered in his eyes like sunlight bouncing off a clear mountain pool. "See if you can resist. If you can't, feel free to play with either of the others. They're not quite as lethal."

"Gee, thanks." She'd procrastinated as long as she could. Time to see how their relationship would handle this first little hiccup. "Tell me something, Mathias. What does your client want with Lynn?"

"Sorry. That's confidential information."

"I see. In other words, it's fine for me to betray a confidence, but not for you."

She could tell he hadn't considered it from that angle before. He frowned, adjusting one of the files on his desk. Apparently it had been a half millimeter off center. "You're right, of course. I don't know why that didn't occur to me before."

She shrugged. "You're too focused on your particular problem. Lots of people do that. It's sort of like looking at a painting."

His gaze flashed to hers, sharp as a laser. "A painting?"

"Sometimes people spend so much time studying the individual details of a piece of art, they forget to step back and look at the big picture."

"That's an interesting comparison." He hesitated, then asked, "Are you interested in art?"

"Sure. Isn't everyone?"

He started to say more, but then apparently changed his mind. "About Lynn..."

"Don't get sidetracked, right?"

He inclined his head. "We can discuss art another time."

There it was again—that reference to the future. "Okay. Let's stick with Lynn. Mathias…" She glanced at him unhappily. "I can't tell you what she said. If that causes problems between us, then I'm sorry. But I'm not going to change my mind."

"In that case, why don't we do what you suggested, and look at the big picture?"

"All right." She approached, perching beside him on his desk. "You have a client that wants something from Lynn. Is that about right?"

"Close enough."

"And you need to know whether or not Lynn is agreeable to giving your client whatever it is he or she wants."

"Exactly."

"But you can't tell me what it is and I can't tell you what Lynn said. Is that about the size of it?"

"'Fraid so."

"Why can't your client approach Lynn directly?"

Again Mathias hesitated, choosing his words with care. "She's afraid."

Jacq blinked in astonishment. "Of Lynn?"

He offered a crooked smile. "Crazy, isn't it?"

"Is there any chance I could meet this client of yours?"

"None."

She didn't take offense. "Well, then there's only one option. We need Lynn to tell you what she told me."

"Is that likely?"

"Not really," Jacq confessed. "But I'll do what I can."

"I'd appreciate that."

A soft knock sounded at the door and Mrs. White poked her head in. "I'm so sorry to interrupt, Mr. Blackstone. Mrs. Car—" She flashed Jacq a harried look. "I mean, your two o'clock is here early. She's terribly upset. I took her into the conference room as you requested, but I'm afraid she's going to run off if you don't come right away."

"I'll be along in a minute." Mathias glanced at Jacq. "I'm sorry about this. We'll have to postpone our conversation."

"No problem. I'll see myself out."

"You don't mind?"

"Not at all."

Mathias slipped his hand around the back of her head and gave her a swift kiss. He started to release her, then hesitated, his gaze consuming hers. His mouth returned and he deepened the kiss. She clung to him for several long minutes until reluctantly, he released her. For an instant neither of them moved, a look of perfect understanding passing between them. "I'll call you," he said. And then he left the room.

Jack picked up her satchel with a sigh and jiggled it. The glass jars inside bumped against each other, emitting a melodic clatter, a sound that never failed to soothe her. She'd transferred the paints from tubes into glass jars, an admitted eccentricity. But she found them easier to mix that way when she was away from home and less of a mess to clean up afterward. She frowned, bouncing the bag against her thigh as she considered her next move.

They really hadn't resolved anything, and they wouldn't unless she figured out how to get Lynn talking. Mathias was still as black-and-white as ever and unlikely to change anytime soon. The jars continued to tinkle merrily, giving her an idea. Well, there was one thing she could do for him before she left.

She could bring a little color into his world.

It didn't take long. Having sketched so many dragons over the past couple days helped the job go much faster. Hardly any time at all passed before she finished. Gazing at his desk in satisfaction, she put away her paints and carefully uncapped the long glass jar she used to store her wet brushes until she could get them home for a proper cleaning.

How long would it take Mathias to notice? she couldn't help but wonder. And how would he react when he did? A tiny smile crept across her mouth. Too bad she wouldn't be able to witness it.

Mrs. White's muffled shriek brought Mathias's head up with a jerk.

"Oh, my heavens," she said with a gasp. "Oh, Mr. Blackstone, I don't know what to say. Really I don't."

Mathias shifted his papers aside and fixed his secretary with a cool gaze. "Calm down, Ebbie. You don't know what to say about what?"

"About... About *that*!" She pointed toward one end of his desk. "This is all my fault. I never should have left her alone in your office."

Mathias shoved back his chair and stood. Circling the desk, he paused at the far corner and stared in amazement. How could he have overlooked this? He'd been sitting not four feet away from it for the past hour. Of course, it could only be the work of one person. And it didn't take much guesswork to figure out who that person might be. The style was too distinctive to mistake.

Jack Rabbitt had painted a baby dragon on his desk.

"I'll get it cleaned off this instant," Mrs. White promised.

Mathias sighed. "If you do, I'm afraid I'll be forced to fire you, Ebbie."

"You want me to leave it there?" she questioned in disbelief. "But...why?"

"It's an original piece of artwork."

A stunning piece of original artwork. Damn, but she was talented. She'd painted the baby dragon a rich, ruby red, the delicate scales tipped in gold. It appeared to be climbing onto the corner of his desk, it's gold claws skittering across the glass, leaving tiny scratch marks in their wake. Through the glass, he could see the creature's underbelly, one foot plastered to the bottom of the desk, the other stretched out and clinging to the far edge. A snakelike tail curled up onto the desk at right angles to the body, the spadelike tip anchored deep into the glass. She'd even painted tiny cracks and gouges around the embedded tail. They looked so real, he ran his finger over them just to prove to himself they weren't.

But the best part of all was the expression on the dragon's face. Mischievous. Daring. Brash. The emerald eyes mocked him, glittering with laughter, and a forked tongue lolling out of the side of its mouth. He knew that expression. He'd seen it on children's faces the world over as they attempted a new and difficult skill.

For a brief time, he'd seen it on his son's face.

"Ebbie?" he whispered.

"Yes, sir?"

"I'd like you to take the rest of the afternoon off."

"Mr. Blackstone?"

"And catch the lights as you go."

"Yes, sir. Right away." Without another word, she

turned and slipped from the room, flicking light switches as she went.

Mathias closed his eyes. Damnation. He'd worked so long and hard to bury the memories where they couldn't touch him anymore, just as he'd fought to close off that part of himself. It was either that or go insane. And with one simple painting, Jacq had brought the memories bursting to the surface, forcing him to face those dark, impossibly bleak days.

Christopher!

His hands clenched. How he missed him. Missed that bright, silly grin. Missed those huge mischievous eyes and tumble of black curls. Missed the impulsive hugs and wet, sticky kisses. One painting. One nonsensical painting and it all came back as if it were yesterday. As though sensing his anguish, Nemesis leaped onto his lap and gave a plaintive meow.

Mathias took a deep cleansing breath, fighting for control. Then he took another. And another. He focused on the rhythm of his breathing, struggling to get past the images trapped in his mind. But there was only one way he could do that.

He gave up the battle for control and allowed the images to come, allowed the pain to consume him. After he'd gone through each precious memory, he envisioned a strongbox and put the pictures inside. Then he locked the box and reburied it in the far reaches of his mind. Buried it deep where it couldn't touch him.

When he was done, he opened his eyes again and looked once more at Jacq's painting. This time he was able to study it objectively. Mathias sighed, realizing there couldn't be any further doubt.

Here before his eyes was confirmation of Jacq's identity.

"So what do I do now, Nemesis?" he murmured, stroking the short yellow fur.

Forty-eight hours ago he'd have known the answer. He'd have moved on to the second stage in the process, the same as always. His procedures were very carefully defined, steps he'd honed and perfected over the years. The first step was to confirm the authenticity of the object or person in question. Once he'd accomplished that, he proceeded to step two—find the best way to approach the subject. The final step often proved the most difficult—to get his hands on what he'd been hired to procure.

He doubted Jacq would make that last step easy for him.

"We'll have to find out why she keeps her identity a secret and how we can get her to give it up," he said at last.

Nemesis flexed his claws.

Mathias shook his head. "No, my friend. Force won't work."

His preferred method in situations such as this—the direct approach—wouldn't succeed, either. He'd tried that already when he'd contacted her agent and made the original request. He'd been turned down flat. No exceptions and no explanations. So, until he determined a workable alternative, he'd have to proceed very, very carefully. This was too vital a procurement to blow.

He drummed his fingers on his desk. What he needed to uncover was Jacq's weak spot, to find her greatest need. Once he knew that, he'd be in a position to bargain—he could make a procurement in exchange for what she'd be giving up. Of course, finding that weak spot would take careful and meticulous planning.

He tossed a legal pad on his desk, careful to keep it

clear of the baby dragon's claws. He knew of only one way to hold Jacq's full attention while he completed his analysis. So, she thought he lacked spontaneity, did she? No problem. He could ''plan'' enough spontaneity to satisfy even her exacting requirements.

Uncapping his pen, he wrote across the top, ''Spontaneous Activities Guaranteed To Capture Jack Rabbitt.''

CHAPTER FIVE

FOR the first time in months, Jacq left the phone plugged in. She didn't bother rationalizing the decision. She knew why she'd made it. She hoped Mathias would call.

And he did—waking her at the crack of dawn the next morning.

"I just got into the office," he announced without preliminary.

She fluffed her pillows behind her and cradled the receiver against her ear. "Am I your first call? I'm flattered," Jacq said, her sleepiness vanishing the instant she heard his distinctive voice. Angelica lifted her head from the nest of covers, her ears twitching.

"You should be. I haven't even had my coffee yet."

She released a low whistle. "The situation with Lynn must be more urgent than I realized."

"This isn't about Lynn," came his terse reply.

"Then what is it about?"

There was a curious silence before he said, "I'm not quite certain. But I think we should find out. Don't you?"

Without question. "What do you suggest?"

"That we get together again. I have several projects I'm working on. Since you enjoyed our evening with the Davenports so much, I thought you'd be interested in trying your hand at another procurement or two."

Interested? She found the idea incredibly appealing. The Davenports's party had been fun. A lot of fun. Still... Mathias never did anything without a reason.

"There isn't an ulterior motive behind your offer, is there?" she teased.

Again came that odd silence, as though he were analyzing her words for any hidden meaning. "What sort of ulterior motive?" he asked, his tone composed and nonchalant. Too nonchalant.

She sighed. "You're hoping that once I have an opportunity to watch you work, I'll change my mind about Lynn, right?"

He swore beneath his breath. "Jacq—"

It took all her self-control not to laugh. "You're doing it again, aren't you?" she cut in.

"Killing two birds with one stone? Sorry. It's second nature."

"Then let me warn you, I won't change my mind about Lynn. Now that we've cleared up that little misunderstanding, do you still want my help?"

"You're forgetting. My procurement problem is only one of the reasons I invited you today."

"And the other reason?"

This time there was no caution. No hesitation. Nothing but a rough, aggressive voice that stated, "I wanted to."

Her reply came just as swiftly. "In that case, I accept. I'd love to help with your next project."

"When can you come by?"

"I'll have to fit in a visit around my work schedule." Not that that would be any problem. With the preliminary manuscript on her "dragon" story finished, that just left the rough sketches for the "dummy" book to complete. She wouldn't start on the actual paintings until she'd received final approval from her editor and art director. And her agent would contact her when that happened. "I'll come by after lunch if that's okay?"

"Come by for lunch," he ordered. "We'll eat together and then you can sit in on my one o'clock appointment."

"Your client won't mind?"

"It's not a confidential matter."

"Oh." That was a relief. "I'll aim for noon."

"Good. I'll see you at twelve. And Jacq?"

"Yes?"

"Thanks for coming."

"My pleasure," she replied with a silly little grin.

Returning the receiver to the cradle, she hopped out of bed. He hadn't mentioned the baby dragon she'd painted on his desk, she suddenly realized. It would be interesting to see if the ever-efficient Mrs. White had cleaned it off or if Mathias had allowed it to stay.

"Well, what do you think, Angel?" Jacq asked as she headed for the shower.

Angelica slinked into the bathroom voicing her opinion in no uncertain terms.

"If my baby dragon's still there, it means he's ready to allow a little color into his life." She yanked her nightgown over her head and tossed it on the floor. "Right?"

Angelica meowed in agreement, assuming her "throne" on top of the toilet seat lid. Only a cat could look so intelligent while sitting on such a perch, Jacq decided with a smile.

"But if it's been washed off," she continued, turning the water on full blast, "I should bring a fast end to a short relationship. Is that about the size of it?"

The cat's tail twitched aggressively.

"Hmm. I was afraid you'd agree. Considering my reaction to his kiss, I suspect *that* will be easier said than done." Jacq stepped into the shower, then poked her head around the curtain as a thought occurred to her. "Which reminds me! You've completely forgotten about Mathias. Knowing him, he'll have a word or two to say about ending our relationship. And I doubt any of them will be pleasant."

At that, Angelica blinked in wise acknowledgment of such an indisputable fact.

Jacq did her best to get to Mathias's office on time. She came close—she was only thirty-five minutes late. But those thirty-five minutes seemed to cause Mrs. White a great deal of concern.

"He's been waiting," she said with a severe frown.

"I would have gotten here sooner, but I saw these in a store window and had to stop." Jacq upended one of the huge plastic bags she held. Vivid rose and jade pillows tumbled onto the dove gray carpet. "Aren't they great?"

"I really don't think—"

"Don't think. Just look." She tossed them onto the couch and stepped back to assess her handiwork. The room was instantly transformed from coldly formal, to brightly welcoming.

Mrs. White sank into her seat. "My goodness," she said faintly.

"And if I just add this..."

From her second bag, Jacq pulled an assortment of silk flowers traversing the full spectrum of colors. She tucked them at random among the white and gray blooms already residing in the huge black floor vases. Stepping back, she admired the results. The vivid array lent a sunny ambience to the room that had been missing before, she decided. It made the reception area downright homey.

"I don't know what Mr. Blackstone will say," Mrs. White fussed. "I really don't. He doesn't take well to colors."

"Mr. Blackstone will learn to take to them," Jacq replied firmly. "And I'll help."

"Now that I don't doubt," Mathias commented in a resigned voice. He stood in the doorway of his office scrutinizing the pillows and flowers. Emotion rippled beneath the surface of his calm green gaze, but whether he felt annoyance or amusement she wasn't quite certain. "You couldn't resist, could you?" he asked.

"'Fraid not." She swept the empty bags off the floor and approached. "Shall I return it all to the store?"

He looked again at the vibrant additions, then slowly shook his head. "Leave them there."

She knew then—without a single, solitary doubt—that the baby dragon still struggled to pull himself onto Mathias's slippery glass-topped desk.

Her smile was positively blinding. He responded with a smile of his own, one full of warmth and possession. One that started that odd tingle in the tips of her toes. It flashed upward, just as it did when he kissed her, shocking her so badly that she jumped.

"It shouldn't happen like that," she told him in an astonished undertone. "You're not even touching me."

"You shouldn't have been late," he responded gravely. "You built up quite a charge."

"Hmm. You could be right. Imagine if I'd been this late and we'd..." Her gaze strayed to his mouth and a warning tingle started in her toes again. "Have I kept you waiting very long?" she hastened to ask.

"Longer than you'll ever know."

There was no mistaking the expression in his eyes this time. The ice had temporarily melted, leaving behind a sizzling heat more potent than a live electrical wire. She stared, unable to look away. Why couldn't she get the color of his eyes right? she wondered helplessly. Perhaps because they changed with his moods—shifting from stormy arctic seas one minute, to a calm mountain pool the next, before burning with hot incandescent green sparks. She liked the sparks best of all.

He glanced past her to his secretary. "Warn me when my one o'clock arrives."

"Yes, sir. I'll put them in the conference room. They just called to say they're running late."

"That's convenient," Jacq said as she stepped into Mathias's office.

"Very convenient," he concurred. "Because it gives me the opportunity to do this...."

The minute the doors closed between the reception area and his office, his mouth captured hers. Then his arms locked around her and he leaned into her as though he couldn't tolerate so much as a breath of air between them. Her satchel of paints hit the floor with a melodic clatter and the plastic bags swirled around their ankles.

"Oh, Mathias," she whispered against his mouth. "You may have cured me."

He pulled back slightly. "Cured you? Of what?"

"I may never be late again." Her eyes fluttered closed. "Not if it means missing something like that."

"Good." Pure masculine frustration punctuated his words. "Because I don't think I could have lasted much longer without kissing you."

He cupped her face and kissed her over and over, his lips hard and heavy on hers. It wasn't enough. Not nearly enough. Her lips parted beneath the avid onslaught and she issued a soft sigh of welcome. He didn't wait for a second invitation. His tongue followed the velvety path inward in the sweetest of invasions.

It had never been like this with a man, she decided hazily. Not ever. She no longer felt a tingle when he touched her. It now felt like she'd caught the raw end of a live wire. It burned, arcing from lips to breast to belly before exploding outward in ever-intensifying waves.

His hands slipped from her face, bunching in the back of her sweater. He wanted her, she was certain, wanted her in the most basic way possible. But she knew he wouldn't act on that desire, no matter how hard-ridden he became. Not until the time was right. Not until she was ready to meet him on equal ground. His kind wasn't interested in submission. His kind respected strength and integrity.

His kind... Her dragon.

With a small murmur, she buried her face in the crook of his shoulder, fighting for breath. He was such a study in contrasts. Precise, yet intense. Fiercely determined, yet considerate. Always in command and yet living at the edge of chaos. Instinctive and urbane, he had a dragon's passion governed by a cool, exacting intellect. Right now, she held the dragon in her arms. But that wouldn't last much longer. Already she sensed his fight for control, felt him gathering his inner reserves to restore order to his universe.

"You're not going to get any lunch if we don't stop," he muttered.

Reluctantly she opened her eyes. "If you're asking which I prefer..." She touched her swollen mouth with the tip of her tongue.

He gave his full attention to the enticing movement. "I know which *I* prefer. Unfortunately, we have too little time to indulge that particular preference and too much time to take this any further without Mrs. White walking in at an inopportune moment.''

"Then I guess we'd better settle for lunch,'' she reluctantly agreed.

He found her mouth once more in a brief, hard caress. "Just for future reference, are you always late for appointments?"

"Always." She reached up to straighten his tie. "It's one of my more endearing qualities."

He offered a wry smile. "That's what I was afraid of. This might be a good time to set a few ground rules."

"Rules." Uh-oh. This didn't sound good.

"Right. Rules. You know, parameters that help define our relationship."

Definitely bad news. "Perhaps I should warn you that I'm not much of a rules and regulations sort of person." She shot him a worried glance. "I guess you hadn't noticed that about me."

"Believe it or not, I had noticed," he said gently. "But I'll try and keep the rules nice and simple and easy to follow."

"What happens if I break one?"

"Don't panic. You won't break any."

Her expression turned grim. "That's what they all say."

He didn't seem terribly concerned by her confession. "I'm sure. I'm also sure you've been quick to correct that misconception."

"Oh, I excel at it," she informed him darkly.

Laughter flickered in his gaze. "In that case, all I ask is that you do your best with these rules. Fair enough?"

"I suppose," she said without much enthusiasm.

"First. Call if you're going to miss a date altogether. Otherwise I'll expect you when I see you."

She blinked in surprise. "Really? No time limits like—if you're not here in ten minutes I go without you?"

He lifted an eyebrow. "Would a time limit work?"

"No," she admitted with brutal honesty.

"Somehow I didn't think so."

"When I'm working I tend to lose track of everything but what I'm doing," she felt obligated to explain. "But that doesn't stop some people from trying to turn me into a clock-watcher."

His mouth tightened ever so slightly. "I'm not 'some people'."

As if she could possibly mistake that not-so-minor detail. "What's rule number two?"

"Rule number two. I'll be where I say, when I say. If we miss each other, I'll give you my pager number. You can call me and we'll make new arrangements." He tucked an escaped curl behind her ear. "Now, are you ready to eat?"

"That's it?" she asked cautiously. "No other ground rules? No other parameters to worry about?"

"That's it. Unless you have a rule or two you'd like to add?"

"Not a one," she said in relief. "What's for lunch? I'm starved."

"Somehow I thought you might be."

He steered her toward where their meal awaited. Catching sight of the small table he indicated, she stumbled to a halt and stared. She'd never seen such an exquisite setting. The sight filled her with helpless confusion.

She smoothed a corner of the snowy damask table-cloth. "You did all this for me?" she managed to ask.

"I did it for us."

"For us." She hugged the words close, enchanted by the implication. "Is—is any of this food in season?"

"Champagne is always in season."

She laughed, waving a hand to indicate several of the dishes. "I meant the lobster and strawberries."

"I was afraid it might be the only meal you ate today. So I went a little overboard." He'd sidestepped a direct response, but she couldn't bring herself to call him on it. "I ordered the meal catered by House Milano. Are you familiar with them? As far as I'm concerned they're the best restaurant in Seattle."

"They provided everything? Even the Limoges?" She cautiously fingered the fine gold banding that edged the eggshell-thin plate. "It's almost museum quality."

"I suspect it's from Joe Milano's private collection."

Her gaze drifted to the crystal and cutlery. "And are the Lalique champagne flutes and Gorham silver from his private collection, too?" Mathias gave a careless shrug and her brows drew together. "This can't be part of their standard service."

"I told him I wanted the best."

"And he gave it to you."

"He owes me a favor or two."

His comment gave her an odd pang. "So you used up one of those favors on me?" His silence was all the confirmation she needed. "No one's ever done anything like this for me before," she murmured.

"Then it's time they did."

She bowed her head, totally overwhelmed. He must have sensed her confusion, for he bent and gave her a kiss of such warmth and gentleness it brought tears to her eyes. Their lips clung and she knew in that instant that their relationship had undergone an unmistakable change. From the beginning they'd connected. But this was something else, something that touched deep within, that reached to that inner self she protected with such zeal. In that timeless moment, the barriers she'd spent so long erecting, tumbled. His name slipped out, filled with vibrant longing.

His mouth caressed hers a final time. "I want you. You know that, don't you?"

She didn't back away from the question, but fixed him with a candid gaze. "Yes, I know. Because it's how I feel, too."

For a brief instant the darkness consuming him eased, revealing a man of indomitable strength and integrity, of depth and determination. "Then I can wait until a more appropriate time to continue this." A hard smile broke across his face as he released her. "But it won't be easy."

"Would lunch help?" she dared to tease.

"Possibly." He held out a chair. "Why don't we start with champagne? I don't know about you, but I could use a drink."

"Yes, please." Perhaps it would help calm the turmoil he'd stirred. She eyed the striking planes of his face. On the other hand, it could make it worse.

He filled her flute, then turned his attention to serving a selection from the various covered dishes. "I think you'll like my next client," he said, the change of subject giving her time to regain her composure. "I look forward to introducing you."

Her gaze feasted on the chilled lobster he piled on her plate. "Now I'm really sorry I'm late. I can eat fast."

"I don't want you to eat fast. I want you to enjoy

your lunch. If my clients arrive before you're through, you can join us later.''

''Do they know I'll be sitting in on the meeting?''

''Of course.'' A quick grin flashed across his mouth. ''I told them my fiancée would be helping me with their problem.''

She could hardly believe it. ''You told them I'm your fiancée?''

''If I didn't, I'm sure you would have,'' he retorted. ''Try the spinach and artichoke dip. It's a specialty of House Milano. Have you ever eaten there?''

''I had a date to go, but we never quite made it.''

''We?''

''My former fiancé and I.'' She managed a careless smile. ''The one before you.''

Fire and ice flared to life in his eyes once again. ''I gather he's no longer a concern?'' Mathias questioned mildly.

''No, he's not.'' She pushed the unpleasant memory aside and sampled the dip. ''Oh, this is wonderful!''

''I'm glad you like it.'' He gave her a moment to enjoy her lunch before asking, ''Was your former fiancé also the one who set the time limits?''

''Time limits, schedules, a whole list of requirements.'' She stabbed her fork into a succulent piece of lobster. ''He had far more rules than you. And it annoyed him no end when I'd break them.''

''Did you break them deliberately?''

Amusement had filtered into his voice and she sent him a look of indignation. ''No. I really tried to follow his silly rules. But it didn't work.''

''I gather it wasn't an amicable parting.''

''It was awful,'' she said flatly. ''Perhaps if my

mother had been alive, it wouldn't have been so bad. I suspect she'd have seen through him from the start.''

''Did the rest of your family like him?''

She grimaced. ''They adored him. Everyone thought he'd be the perfect husband for me.''

''I wonder why they thought that?'' His idle tone was at direct odds with the grim look darkening his expression.

She gave the safest possible answer. ''I don't know.''

Mathias reached out and caught her hand. ''Yes, you do,'' he said, refusing to let her evade the truth. ''They thought he'd be perfect because he'd accomplish what they'd failed to. He'd bring you into line.''

She attempted a careless shrug. ''If it makes you feel any better, they paid a steeper price than me for trusting him. After he left I realized I couldn't change my nature and shouldn't try. So you might say my dear ex-fiancé did me a favor by dumping me.''

She could tell he had a thousand questions he wanted answered. To her surprise, he didn't ask them, choosing instead to turn the conversation in a new direction. ''Since you're not like your father, I have to assume you take after your mother.''

Jacq nodded. ''I look like her and our personalities are similar.''

''You were thirteen when she died?''

''A week shy of my thirteenth birthday.'' She didn't bother asking how he knew. According to J.J. he knew everything about everyone. She slanted a surreptitious glance toward his desk. A telltale splash of red glistened in the corner. Well... He knew almost everything. ''J.J. had just turned ten and Cord was only eight.''

''And you did your best to try and fill your mother's role in the family.'' It wasn't a question.

"I tried…and failed miserably. Within a few weeks of her death I'd turned all of our clothing an interesting shade of either pink or blue because I kept putting colored clothes in with the whites."

"I suspect you were the only one who didn't mind."

She gave him a crooked smile. "Good guess. And then there were the meals. They were the worst part. Either I'd forget to take something out of the freezer or I'd forget to take it out of the oven. As soon as Dad realized I couldn't handle the responsibility, he hired a housekeeper."

"He should have done that right from the start instead of making you feel like a failure," Mathias bit out.

She realized then that she'd been far too frank. He was absolutely, down-to-the bone furious. She'd never realized anger could look so cold. The ice burned in his gaze and hardened his expression. For the first time she understood why her family considered Mathias so intimidating. She shivered, hoping he never had cause to direct that controlled fury her way.

"Dad wouldn't do anything to hurt me," she insisted, hoping to deflect his anger. Having Mathias upset with her father wouldn't be in Limelight's best interest, she belatedly realized. "Not on purpose."

"Nevertheless, he put a huge burden on a young child."

"You have to understand that it wasn't a good time for any of us. No one was thinking very straight." She struggled to explain what those dark days had been like. "It took everything we had just to get through each day without Mom. Dad grew more and more focused on business. Without her tempering influence, he became totally rules-and-regulations-oriented. J.J. and Cord had no problem following in his footsteps. But I..." She shrugged, trailing off.

"No grids for you."

A quick smile came and went. "No grids."

"And you'd lost the one person who understood you." To her relief, his anger had eased.

"I had my grandmother. She understood. But she didn't want to interfere in my relationship with my father. She felt we should work things out between us." Until the end. Until Jacq had nowhere else to turn.

"I'm beginning to regret having made even two rules for you to follow," he said.

"Really?" His confession delighted her. "If it makes you feel any better, I think there's a real possibility that I'll be able to handle them. At least you're not trying to change me."

"No," he said gently. "I like you just the way you are."

A soft burr sounded from the direction of his desk. Excusing himself, Mathias went to answer the phone. "Thank you, Ebbie. Offer them soft drinks. I'll be there in a few minutes."

"Your clients have arrived?" Jacq frowned, torn between two temptations—lunch and this latest procurement.

"There's no rush. Finish eating," Mathias insisted. "Oh, and one more thing." He reached into his pocket and pulled out a small box. Crossing to where she sat, he flipped open the lid and removed a ring. "For you."

She couldn't believe it. "I—I don't understand."

He lifted her left hand and slipped the heavy band onto her ring finger. "I can't have you running around telling everyone you're my fiancée without the proof to go along with it." Then he bent and kissed her.

Before she could react, he was gone.

She stared in shock at her finger. It couldn't be! A magnificent golden dragon clung there, its tail wrapping in circles all the way to her knuckle. Two fiery emeralds formed the eyes and it held a ruby heart clutched fast in its claws. She'd never seen anything so beautifully crafted, with such attention to detail. There was only one difference between this ring and the one she'd described at the Davenports's.

This one fit.

Jacq didn't know how long she sat there, lost in thought. When she finally awoke to her surroundings it was because the urge to find Mathias surpassed every other need. Only the knowledge that she wouldn't find him alone kept her from dashing from the room. She glanced again at the ring. Of course, she couldn't keep it. But perhaps she could find another way of expressing her appreciation.

Her gaze shifted to his desk and she walked slowly toward it. She thought she'd caught a glimpse of red earlier. Sure enough, the baby dragon still clung to the edge of the glass. Mathias had repositioned his files and papers so they didn't encroach on the dragon's territory and it gave her an idea.

She glanced toward the door, aware that she didn't have long. She was expected in the conference room soon and she had to admit—she was quite excited at the idea of helping with another procurement. Perhaps this time there wouldn't be a confidentiality problem. Pulling out tiny jars of paint, she frowned, considering the Davenport situation. There had to be a way she could obtain the information Mathias needed without betraying Lynn's confidence. It would just take some thought.

A short time later, Jacq finished her latest additions to

the desk. Packing away her paints and brushes, she studied her handiwork, wondering whether he'd say anything this time. If he didn't, she'd just keep adding to it. Considering how well he understood her personality, perhaps he'd also understand that this was her way of sharing herself with him.

CHAPTER SIX

Mathias spent the next half an hour going over his clients's request. As he discussed the situation with them, he waited for a familiar footstep, waited to hear an impetuous knock, followed by that husky, full-bodied laugh. What was it about Jacq that stirred such anticipation—that made him long to see a mop of gold-streaked curls poke around the open door and her mischievous, angled face fill up with a smile?

"Well, can you do it?" Patsie demanded in her typically forthright manner.

Mathias willed himself to concentrate on the task at hand. "You need to narrow the focus of your request some more," he replied. Although this particular procurement wasn't in the least complicated, he took his time so Jacq would have an opportunity to join them. He knew she'd be disappointed if she missed out. "Make a list of what you want and put it in the order of most important to least."

"I'll write everything down," Dana offered, tucking a lock of seal-brown hair behind her ear.

Just then Jacq breezed into the room. "Sorry I'm late," she said, offering the smile he'd spent the past half hour envisioning. "What have I missed?"

She still wore his ring, Mathias noted, and a fierce satisfaction seized hold. "This is my fiancée, Jacq Randell." He made the introductions. "She'll be working with me on your request. Jacq, this is Dana Ramsey and Patsie Tolson. They're both fourteen and best friends. They're also about to become sisters.''

Jacq held out her hand to each in turn, never revealing by so much as a flicker of an eyelash that she found the two a surprise. ''It's a pleasure to meet you. What can I do to help?'' she asked, taking the chair next to his.

''We want to give our parents a honeymoon,'' Patsie said. ''And we're making a list of possibilities. We'd love to send them to Hawaii or Alaska, but we've only saved two hundred and twelve dollars. So we'll have to settle for whatever we can buy with that.''

Dana finished making a notation on her pad and glanced up with a frown. ''We would have saved more, but we didn't find out in time.''

Catching Jacq's look of confusion, Mathias explained, ''Dana's mother and Patsie's father are getting married. The girls were told that a honeymoon was out of the question because of work complications.''

''What a crock that turned out to be!'' Patsie snorted, her bright red hair falling forward to graze a freckled cheek.

''Hey, you believed it, same as me,'' Dana said. ''If we hadn't overheard them talking last week, we'd never have learned the truth.''

''What truth is that?'' Jacq asked, glancing from one to the other.

''Instead of having a honeymoon, they're putting the money toward our college tuition.'' Patsie jumped to her feet and began pacing. ''The minute we discovered that, we both took after-school jobs so we could give them a honeymoon as a joint Christmas and wedding present.''

''I just wish we'd known sooner so we could have saved more,'' said Dana. She peeked at Mathias from beneath her lashes. ''When we read about your granting

Christmas wishes, we decided to call and see if this was something you'd be willing to help us with.''

Jacq shot Mathias a startled look. "Christmas wishes?''

Damn. He hadn't intended for her to find out about that. At least, not yet. "I'll explain later,'' he said easily, then returned his attention to the two girls. "I assume you have some ideas for this honeymoon.''

"It has to be romantic,'' Dana said thoughtfully. "Like a mountain hideaway or a fancy hotel or something.''

"We'd like it to have a fireplace and a Jacuzzi or whirlpool, if possible,'' Patsie added, peering over Dana's shoulder at the official list. "Someplace where they can be private.''

"And flowers, if we can afford it.''

"And champagne. Definitely champagne.''

"When are they getting married?'' Jacq asked.

"Christmas night.'' Dana sighed. "Isn't that romantic?''

Jacq locked gazes with Mathias, amusement stirring in her eyes. "I have it on excellent authority that Christmas is the most romantic time of all to be married.''

"That's what we think, too. Which is why Patsie and I want them to have a honeymoon. It just wouldn't be right, otherwise.''

"I tried to make a reservation myself,'' Patsie claimed with a touch of indignation. "But no one would let me. They all said I was too young and needed to have an adult handle it.''

Jacq didn't hesitate. "We'll be happy to take care of the arrangements. Won't we, Mathias?''

He suppressed a smile. His fiancée's quixotic nature

didn't surprise him in the least, though he doubted she'd appreciate having the more predictable aspects of her personality pointed out. Not when she prided herself on spontaneity.

"Mathias?" she prompted, nudging him with a sharp little elbow.

He winced. He'd definitely have to break her of that habit before she fractured a damned rib. "Of course we'll help," he hastened to say.

"Mathias is excellent at research," she confided to the girls. "He'll find the perfect honeymoon location, I promise."

"We're still trying to earn more money," Dana said earnestly. "But considering how little we've managed to save, I'm afraid we'll have to settle for someplace wonderful instead of someplace spectacular."

Jacq waved her hand, dismissing Dana's concern. "You let us worry about the financial end of things. Just leave us your list and we'll get right to work on it. Won't we, Mathias?"

He didn't wait for the elbow this time. "Oh, absolutely."

The two girls grinned in delight. "This is great!" Patsie exclaimed. "Thank you so much."

Mathias stood. "Give us a couple days to check into your request." He shook hands with each of the girls. "I'll be in touch before the end of the week and we'll go from there."

Chattering excitedly, the girls left. Mathias glanced at Jacq, waiting for her comments. She sat at the table, studying the list Dana had concocted with single-minded intensity. After a few minutes she looked up, enthusiasm tinting her eyes the rich golden amber of autumn leaves.

"Giving their parents a honeymoon is such a sweet idea," she said. "Won't this be fun helping?"

"I thought you might enjoy it."

"Let's get to work right away. Where should we start?" She snapped her fingers. "I know. I'll contact a travel agency. Or maybe I could check the ads in the newspaper. They always run lots of holiday packages."

Mathias shook his head. "Not so fast, sweetheart. You're forgetting a step or two."

Her brows drew together. "What steps?" she asked warily.

"First we confirm their identities and the facts they've given us."

"You're kidding."

"'Fraid not. It's vital that we make sure they've told us the truth. We also need to ascertain whether or not this is a wish their parents would like to have granted."

"How can you doubt it?" she questioned in astonishment.

"If there's one certainty about people, it's that they're unpredictable." He rested a hip on the table next to her and picked up the list she'd been studying, flicking it with his finger. "By fulfilling this wish, I'm taking a level of control away from Dana and Patsie's parents. I'm making decisions for them that are personal. How would you feel in their position?"

"I think it would depend on the request being made," Jacq replied slowly. "It would also depend on why the person made the request in the first place and what effect the decision would have on me."

"I agree." He returned the list to the table. "Now suppose there's another reason why Mrs. Ramsey or Mr. Tolson have decided against a honeymoon. Dana and Patsie think they've discovered that reason—that it's a financial problem. But what if going on a honeymoon resurrects terrible memories. Or what if one of them really does have work obligations.''

''I never thought about those possibilities,'' Jacq admitted.

''It would be irresponsible to interfere in other people's lives without giving it due consideration.''

''So I'm beginning to realize.'' She sighed. ''Tell me something. How are you going to find out whether or not Patsie and Dana's parents want to go on a honeymoon?''

''First, I'll do a background check on all of them and confirm their identities. I'll also confirm that the parents are getting married. Next I'll investigate their financial status and—''

''You can do all that?'' Jacq interrupted in astonishment.

He lifted an eyebrow. ''Of course.''

''What if everything the girls said is accurate? What then?''

''Then I'll make some discreet inquiries at their parents' places of employment. Once I'm satisfied that the wish is doable, we'll focus on providing the soon-to-be Mr. and Mrs. Tolsons with the perfect Christmas honeymoon.''

Enthusiasm reanimated Jacq's expression. ''And that's where I come in.''

''Yes,'' he said, the corner of his mouth tilting upward. ''That's where you come in.''

''Which reminds me. Dana said something about your granting Christmas wishes. What did she mean by that?''

He hesitated, considering how much to tell her. He didn't like exposing his December activities to public scrutiny. Although it might work to his advantage once he found the right angle for approaching "Jack Rabbitt," he'd rather not use these particular requests as emotional leverage. At least, not if he could help it.

"Certain procurements have to be completed before the end of the year. Dana's is one of them. I guess that's what she meant."

"Oh." A hint of disappointment colored her voice. "I thought maybe you were running around playing Santa or something."

If she only knew. "I don't think he'd appreciate my horning in on his business, do you?"

"That's all right, Mathias," she consoled. "I'm sure you do your best."

"Gee, thanks," he retorted dryly. "It gives 'damned with faint praise' a whole new meaning."

"Only when you're being compared to Santa Claus." Tilting her head to one side, she teased, "You would look fantastic in a red suit, however. No competition there."

He offered a lazy smile. "Most people who know me would agree. Though I suspect the red suit they have in mind comes with a tail, horns and a pitchfork."

Her laughter broke free. "You can't fool me with that one anymore. Others might find you tough and intimidating, but I happen to know it's all an act."

His smile faded. "You're mistaken, sweetheart. It's no act."

"How can you say that?" she scolded. "You work every day helping others. What could be more altruistic?"

As much as he appreciated her faith in him, it would be wrong to allow her to operate under such a delusion. Determination filled him—a determination that she see him for the man he was, instead of the man she'd like him to be.

"You think I'm altruistic?" He shook his head. "Let me set the record straight. My work isn't all fun and games. There are instances when my procurements have caused harm. A lot of harm."

"But you didn't do it deliberately," she protested.

"Yes. On occasion it has been deliberate." The time had come for brutal honesty. "I've turned people away, people who've needed my help."

"Why?"

"Various reasons. With some I chose not to help because their requests were unrealistic or impossible—"

"Or unethical?"

"That, too. Others I couldn't help."

"There's nothing wrong with that."

"Jacq…" He caught hold of her shoulders and pulled her free of the chair and into his arms. "I want you to know the truth. I've ferreted out secrets that individuals have worked hard to keep private—secrets I've then exposed to public scrutiny. I've hidden people whom others want found. And I've used every means at my disposal to tempt men and women into giving up their dearest treasures."

"Why?" she demanded again.

"Because I was paid to." He closed his eyes, stroking the fragile bones beneath his palms. She felt incredible, soft and supple and brimming with a warm vitality. It brought home how much he wanted her—and how likely he was to lose her. "I'm good at what I do, sweetheart. Very good. That's why people come to me, because they know I can get the job done."

"There has to be more to it than that." Desperation

edged her voice. "You wouldn't have made those pro-curements unless it was the right thing to do."

He didn't answer.

"I mean..." Her gaze swept to his face, fastening there with heartrending conviction. "The secrets you re-vealed, they belonged to individuals who'd done some-thing wrong, didn't they?"

"No, Jacq. They were simply secrets that someone paid me to uncover. You of all people should know that secrets aren't always good or bad, right or wrong. And the reasons for exposing those secrets are as numerous as the reasons for keeping them." He spoke urgently, willing her to understand. "That's why I have to be so careful. I have to weigh the potential harm against the potential benefit."

"But the reasons— You said you make procurements only if they're legal and ethical."

"And I do my best. Unfortunately it doesn't always work out that way. Is it unethical to offer a person a huge sum of money to give up a possession that means the world to them? Is it unethical to reveal a secret if it's the truth? I walk a fine line. I do my best. But oc-casionally people are hurt as a result of my interfer-ence."

Alarm filled her gaze and he knew why. He wished he could level with her, wished he could warn her. But that would only defeat his own purpose. If there'd been a more forthright, more honorable solution, he'd have taken it long ago.

"I have to go," she murmured, pulling free of his grasp. "Will you contact me when you're through re-searching Patsie and Dana? In the meantime I'll make a few inquiries with local travel agents."

"Don't put too much work into it until I let you know the results of my investigation."

She lifted her gaze to his. The colors were muted, misted a turbid gray. "I don't need to wait," she insisted.

"Jacq—"

"I'm sure they'll check out just fine." She reached for her satchel. For the first time the glass jars within emitted a harsh rather than melodious jangle. "I know! I'll go ahead and jot down some of the more romantic hideaways I come across."

"Jacq—"

She refused to look at him. "Which reminds me..." She gave her full attention to sorting through the papers scattered across the table. "What did I do with Dana's list? I want to make certain the places I choose have all the necessary requirements—"

He caught hold of her, tugging her back into his arms. "I'm sorry I upset you," he murmured against the top of her head. "I didn't mean to."

The breath left her lungs in a gusty sigh and she burrowed into the crook of his shoulder. "Then why did you?" she asked in a muffled voice.

"You want the truth?"

Her head bobbed up and down, the riot of gold-streaked curls a silken caress along his jaw.

"I guess—" He pushed his response through gritted teeth. "I guess because I was afraid."

She stilled. "Afraid?" She peeked up, studying him with a nerve-racking intensity. "Afraid of what?"

"Afraid that you'd turn me into someone I'm not," he confessed. "Afraid you'd paint a fantasy image of me in your mind. An image I wouldn't have a prayer of living up to."

A tiny smile quivered at the corners of her mouth. "You're afraid I'll paint you all one color?"

"Yeah. I suppose I am."

"So you're determined to convince me that you're not a nice guy, is that it?" The steely gray had faded from her eyes. Now they gleamed with all the clarity of a bright autumn morning, filled with crisp golds and browns and greens. "You don't just procure for the good guys, you also procure for the bad?"

"Something like that."

"Okay. So you've convinced me you're a total louse." Her smile turned to a grin. "Now what?"

He released a gusty sigh. "I'm not a total louse."

"Just half a louse?" she teased.

"Yeah. I guess that about sums it up. Jacq... I need you to understand," he said softly, insistently. "I don't want you to blind yourself to the truth. And in some cases, the truth isn't pretty."

She remained silent for a long moment. Finally she asked, "Have you any regrets, Mathias? I mean... Have you ever taken on a procurement that afterward you were sorry you'd made?"

He thought about it, then shook his head. "No. Some have been tough decisions. A few have been close calls. But I can honestly say that there isn't a single one I regret."

"That's all I needed to know." The last of the clouds cleared from her expression. "By the way, I want to thank you for the ring. It was fun having the opportunity to wear it."

He stopped her before she could remove it. "Leave it on."

"I can't do that. People will think we're really engaged."

"Leave it on."

"Mathias, we're not engaged," she argued. "It wouldn't be right to wear a ring."

"Leave it."

To his relief she gave up, apparently conceding she wasn't going to win this particular argument. At least not at the moment. "I have to admit, I'd love to know how you were able to find a band that matched the one I described."

"It's my job to procure the unusual, remember?"

"But I invented that description." She studied the ring, a tiny frown puckering her brow. "I can't believe you were able to find it."

"I told you. I'm good at my job."

"Maybe I should write that down."

"Maybe this will help you remember." Gathering her into his arms, he bent to kiss her.

She met him halfway, impatience causing her mouth to collide with his. "I know we can do better than that," she said, chuckling at the momentary awkwardness.

"Prove it."

She didn't need any further prompting. Capturing his jaw within her palms, she stroked her thumbs across his lower lip. A groan of pleasure rumbled deep in his chest and she swayed closer. Whispering his name, she kissed him, her lips parting beneath his in sweet eagerness. There was an honest passion about her that stirred him, a sincerity he couldn't mistake. He cupped the nape of her neck, his fingers forking beneath the silken curls.

Her hands slipped from his jaw and she wrapped her arms around his waist, hugging him against her slender curves. The temptation to explore those curves drove him beyond endurance. He wanted to put his mark on her, to make her his. He wanted to carry her off to his penthouse apartment and stay there for as long as it took to turn the fantasy of the ring she wore into reality. But this was one procurement he didn't intend to rush.

Not when it was the most important he'd ever made.

As though sensing his thoughts, she pulled away, fixing him with a serious gaze. "I'd better leave."

"It's not what either of us wants."

"No, it's not. But we'll do it just the same. Won't we?"

"Apparently so." He snatched a final kiss and set her from him. "I'll call you tomorrow. And thanks for your help."

"I enjoyed it. It was fun."

"Be sure you take my coat and umbrella. It looks like rain."

"I was hoping you'd say that." She peeked at him from beneath her lashes, laughter gleaming in her eyes. "In fact... I was counting on it." Planting a final kiss on his jaw, she grabbed her satchel and dashed from the room.

Mathias walked into his office and started toward his desk when he suddenly realized the dragon painted in the corner of the glass top had companions. He detoured to that side and examined the changes, shaking his head in amusement. Jacq had added significantly to the painting. Three naked fairies now frolicked along the edge of the smoked glass just beneath the dragon. A forest had also sprung up, leaves, branches and vines positioned to preserve the winged sprites' modesty. He studied the newly-enlarged painting and grinned. He liked her sense of humor.

The first of the fairies clung to the baby dragon, attempting to help him onto the slippery glass. The second

fairy gripped the first around the waist. The third fairy—
heels threatening to slip out from under her—held fast
to the second fairy's wings, pulling with all her strength.
All three were on the verge of falling flat on their bare
bottoms.

His eyes narrowed as he examined her artwork. There
was something familiar about one of the fairies. Then it
hit him and he chuckled aloud. The last of the three was
the spitting image of Jacq's sister, J.J. The tiny creature
had the same thick cloud of ebony hair, the same fierce
black eyes and the same determined expression. It raised
a very interesting question. Were all of Jacq's books
peopled with familiar faces? And if so, did J.J. know
that she frolicked half-naked through them in the guise
of a fairy? Somehow he doubted that she did. He made
a mental note to check his collection of Jack Rabbitt
books when he returned to his apartment.

"Mr. Blackstone?" Ebbie White slipped into his office, carrying a stack of folders. "These are the last of
the Christmas requests. Oh! My goodness. Your fiancée's been busy, I see."

"Very busy," he concurred.

Ebbie peeked over his shoulder, examining the latest
additions. "She certainly is a talented young lady."

"That she is," he murmured. He took the folders from
his secretary and stacked them on the opposite end of
the desk from the paintings.

"I notice you're reluctant to put anything on top of
them, as well," Ebbie commented. "If Ms. Randell
keeps this up, you'll soon run out of desk space."

A quick grin slashed across his mouth. "I believe
that's the idea."

Amusement dawned in Ebbie's gaze. "It would appear I'm not the only one who thinks you work too hard.''

"I'm not sure that's the point of this particular exercise. Unless I'm mistaken, Jacq's trying to force some color into my life.''

"Thus the pillows and silk flowers and desk-painting.''

"You got it. I believe it's also supposed to make me less grid-oriented.''

"Grid-oriented?''

"I think that's her way of saying less neat and precise.''

Ebbie laughed. "Will it work?''

"I think,'' Mathias admitted with a sigh, "it just might.''

Jacq walked into her cottage and hung Mathias's coat in the hall closet. Angelica trotted over to greet her. Curling her tail around Jacq's ankle, she announced there were messages on the answering machine with a plaintive meow.

There was only one, but it was terse and to the point. "Come up to the house when you get in. We need your help.''

Only Turk could manage to make a request for help sound like an order. Returning to the closet, she grabbed Mathias's coat again. She could have worn one of the several she owned. But she liked wearing his. Even though the sleeves were ridiculously long and she had enough room inside its warm folds for at least two more people, she preferred the simple black wool over any of her more flamboyant garments. And it was for one simple reason—it belonged to Mathias.

Wrapping herself in the protective folds, she inhaled

the woodsy scent of his cologne. The faintest trace still lingered. For some reason, it gave her the fortitude she needed to face her relatives.

She ran the three to ground in the library. "Reporting as ordered," she joked as she entered the room.

As usual, her father ignored her attempt at humor. "Ah, Jacqueline. Thanks for dropping by."

"What's up?" she asked.

"Just a small matter we wanted to run by you," her father replied, getting right down to business. "We hoped to get your take on the situation."

"Is this Limelight business?" she asked, knowing full well it couldn't be anything else.

Her father and J.J. exchanged a quick look. Cord grimaced. It was answer enough.

"You know the agreement we made," she reminded gently.

"And we've kept that agreement," Turk retorted. "But this is serious. We wouldn't have called you otherwise. You know we wouldn't."

"Jacq... I've phoned Blackstone's client a dozen times in an attempt to set up an appointment," J.J. explained. "I can't get past the secretary. We're not asking you to help with the account. We wouldn't do that. All we want is for you to work some of that magic charm of yours and get to the owner."

Jacq frowned. "This doesn't make any sense. This client needs a PR firm, right?"

Turk shrugged. "As far as we know."

"Then why won't he take a meeting?"

No one had an answer.

"All right," Jacq said with a sigh. She slipped off Mathias's coat and tossed it over the arm of a nearby chair. "Give me a name and number. I'll see what I can do."

Cord shoved a piece of paper in her direction. "This is all the information we have."

The paper had a business name, King Investments, and a phone number. J.J. had scrawled the secretary's name at the bottom—Jewel Bright. "That's a joke, right?" Jacq demanded.

Turk shrugged. "Apparently not."

"Well, what's the client's name? Who owns this King Investments?"

"We haven't a clue," her father snapped. "I assume this is Mathias's idea of a test. He wants to see how well we handle the situation. If we pull it off, we're his PR firm of choice. Screw up and we're out. Right now, the chances of our succeeding are fading fast."

"Well, I'll give it a try and see what happens." She crossed to her father's desk, plucked the phone receiver from the cradle and punched in the number.

"King Investments," a sultry voice answered.

"Good afternoon," Jacq said pleasantly. "This is Jacq Randell with Limelight International."

"Yes?"

"I'd like to set up an appointment with your CEO."

"One moment, please." A short time later she returned to the line. "Did you say this was *Jacq Randell* with Limelight International?"

"That's correct."

"I have a few minutes available for you on Friday at three."

"That would be fine," Jacq said evenly. "One more thing... I need your CEO's name."

"I'm so sorry," the secretary replied. "I'm not at liberty to divulge that information."

"Why not?"

"I'm sure my employer will be only too happy to explain on Friday." And with that, the line went dead.

Jacq frowned as she hung up. "I don't like the feel of this," she said, turning to face her father.

"What did the woman say?"

"Very little," she admitted. "All I did was give my name. For some unknown reason, it worked like a charm. You now have an appointment at three on Friday."

"That's great," Cord enthused. But J.J. remained silent, her brow furrowed.

"No, it's not great," Jacq corrected, exchanging a quick look with her sister. "There's something funny about this setup. None of it makes sense. So, if you don't mind my making a suggestion... Be careful. Don't commit to anything. Research the company and the owner before you take this job."

"We've already taken the job, remember?" Turk retorted. "Blackstone warned us that his client requires special attention. He also made it clear that in order to handle any future business, we had to succeed with this account. So no matter what the setup is, we have to take it on. That's all there is to it."

"That isn't all there is," Jacq argued forcefully. "You're forgetting one very important fact. You don't have to take the job. If the owner of King Investments isn't on the up and up, you have every right to refuse to work with him. Sometimes the only right answer is a flat-out no."

"I'm sure once we meet, it will all work out. Thanks for your help, Jacq."

It was clearly a dismissal and she gave in, aware that nothing she said would make a difference. It was up to the Limelighters to deal with the situation. She could only hope her concerns had made an impact on Cord and J.J. "No problem, Dad," she said, pulling on Mathias's coat. "Good luck on Friday."

And with that, she left them to discuss their strategy for handling the mysterious owner of King Investments.

CHAPTER SEVEN

"YOUR cat doesn't like me."

"You're imagining it," Jacq protested. "Angelica loves everyone."

"I'm not imagining it." Mathias pulled onto the car ferry and nosed in close to the car ahead of him. "Angelica took an instant dislike to me. Which brings up another matter. That beast's name is a contradiction in terms."

A tiny frown appeared between Jacq's brows. "What are you talking about? How is it a contradiction in terms?"

He shut off the engine and swiveled in the seat to face her. "You have a black cat named Angelica who did nothing but hiss at me from the moment we were introduced. Any name but the one you chose would have been more suitable. How does Beelzebub grab you?"

She lifted an eyebrow. "What is it with you and names? First Nemesis and now Beelzebub."

"At least Nemesis is a hell of a lot more accurate than what you named your cat."

"Angel is an angel," she protested indignantly. "She wasn't serious when she hissed at you. She was just sizing you up."

"For her next meal, I don't doubt," he muttered, grabbing her overnight bag from the back seat.

Jacq slid from the car and waited while Mathias secured her suitcase in the trunk before explaining, "Angelica's intimidated by dragons. That's all."

115

"Dragons." He slammed the trunk closed and faced her. "I didn't realize you were having a problem with them," he commented dryly. "Have you thought about calling in an exterminator?"

"Don't be ridiculous! I'm not talking about real dragons. I meant you. Once Angelica realizes you aren't going to hurt her, she'll settle right down."

"She thinks *I'm* a dragon? Should I even bother having you explain that?"

"It's my fault," Jacq admitted with a sigh. "I made the mistake of comparing you to a dragon and she hasn't quite come to terms with it yet. Give her time."

He released a silent groan. "I get it. You're one of those pet people."

"Pet people?" Her eyes narrowed. "What's *that* supposed to mean?"

"You know full well what I mean. You're one of those types who act like their pet is a real person, aren't you? You anthropomorphize them."

"I most certainly do not. I'm well aware that my cat is a cat." She folded her arms across her chest. "But she can still have her feelings hurt like the rest of us. And speaking of anthropomorphizing animals... What about Nemesis?"

"What about him?"

"Don't tell me you treat him like a cat."

"Not only do I treat him like a cat, he *is* a cat!" Mathias snagged her elbow and headed for the steps leading to the passenger lounge. "He's an intelligent, affectionate animal who happens to share my taste in women. He's also a hell of a lot better behaved than your beast."

"Angelica has impeccable manners!"

His eyebrow winged upward. "I loved the way she displayed those impeccable manners."

"It was a hair ball," Jacq muttered. "It could have happened to anyone."

"Yeah, right. To anyone wearing Italian leather shoes."

Without question, a change of subject would benefit them both. "I'm so glad Patsie and Dana checked out. This research trip will be a lot of fun."

Aside from slanting her an amused glance, he took the abrupt switch in topic with good grace. "I'm looking forward to it, too. What made you decide on the Olympic peninsula?"

"I thought about finding a mountain hideaway in the Cascades, but this way the Tolsons will have the advantage of both the mountains and the ocean. I even found a listing for an island retreat. I wouldn't mind escaping to an island, would you?"

"It depends on whether or not they have indoor plumbing."

A broad grin spread across her mouth. "You don't like roughing it?"

"Not in December, thank you. And not if I were on my honeymoon. For some strange reason the words honeymoon and room service seem to go together a hell of a lot better than honeymoon, outhouses and cooking dinner on a wood-burning stove."

Her grin faded. "I hadn't thought about that."

"You would have eventually," he reassured. "Does this island getaway come equipped with electricity and central heating?"

"I don't know." She released a sigh of discouragement. "I was really hoping it would work out, though. But maybe we'd better call the rental agent and ask about the amenities. I doubt the Tolsons will want to stay there if it's too primitive."

"Good idea." He opened the door leading to the lounge and gestured for her to proceed. "The imagination often creates a much more attractive picture than reality. That's why I'd like to get a look at these places before we choose."

"You're right. I'd hate to disappoint Patsie and Dana, that's for sure." She played with the leather strap on her satchel, relaxing minimally when she heard the comforting rattle of her paint jars. "I'm trying hard to get this right. Did I tell you that I made a list and everything?"

He stilled. "*You* made a list?"

"Boggles the mind, doesn't it?"

"It certainly does." He wrapped an arm around her shoulder and dropped a quick kiss among the curls at her temple. "And just so you know... You're not going to disappoint them."

She bowed her head. "I never dreamed procuring could be so difficult. But it's a huge responsibility."

"It can be." He captured her chin in his hand, lifting her face. "Hey, cheer up. This is a fun procurement, remember? We've got two whole days to spend together researching the perfect honeymoon. What could be more enjoyable than that?"

She gave it serious consideration. "Nothing that I can think of," she finally admitted, her good humor returning.

"Come on. Let's go outside and see how long we can last before the cold drives us in."

"At least I brought a coat this time."

"I can't begin to tell you how relieved I am to hear that."

"Why?" she teased. "So I won't freeze or because I finally returned yours?"

"As far as I'm concerned, you can keep my damned coat. The only thing I care about is you."

His comment kept her warm for a long time.

Facing the frigid December wind as the ferry rumbled across Puget Sound gave Jacq the perfect excuse to snuggle in Mathias's arms. This past week had been a wonderful experience. She'd spent every single day with Mathias and enjoyed procuring almost as much as painting. Of course, she hadn't given up on her book. She'd worked on both the rough sketches for that as well as adding to Mathias's desk.

It intrigued her that he still hadn't said a word about her artwork. She also found it intriguing that the stacks of files and papers kept shifting so they wouldn't encroach on the fantasy world slowly unfolding across the smoked glass. A tiny smile flirted at the edges of her mouth. What would he do when she finished? Replace the desk?

"I see that smile. What's so funny?" he asked, tucking her more firmly against him.

Deciding to avoid the precise truth, she chose one of the procurements they'd worked on together to blame for her amusement. "I was thinking about Adele Gravis, her house and the Fearsome Foursome," Jacq responded promptly. Mathias had approached Adele for a client interested in purchasing her house—a beautiful Queen Anne mansion that she'd lived in since her newlywed days.

He chuckled. "Ah, yes. The Fearsome Foursome. Adele and her friends were certainly serious about their bridge game, weren't they?"

"Serious? Try ruthless. When I saw the tea service

and lace tablecloth and sponge cake, I figured, 'Oh, how sweet. A friendly little game of bridge.' Then Gladys cut the cards and started spitting them across the table. I never realized anyone could move that fast!''

"She could have taught a Vegas dealer a thing or two,'' Mathias concurred.

"Still… They were all so friendly and they enjoy playing so much. It's a shame they can't get together more often.''

"Oh, really?'' He glanced down at her. "I hadn't heard that. Why can't they?''

"Adele said the other ladies often have trouble finding a ride to her place. I suspect the other three aren't in the same financial position as Adele and can't always afford the cabfare over.''

"That's too bad.''

"Two of the women live in the same retirement home. I suppose Adele could move in with them if there was an opening. It seems a shame, though, to give up a huge, beautiful house in exchange for a tiny little room.'' Jacq caught her lip between her teeth, saying hesitantly, "I can understand why she's reluctant to sell. Can't you?''

He rested his chin on top of her head. "Yes, I can. Unfortunately, that's what my client has hired me to convince her to do.''

She swiveled in his arms, grabbing at the lapels of his coat. "But what if that isn't what Adele wants?'' she protested. "Oh, Mathias, you can't steal the house out from under her!''

His expression darkened. "Who the hell said anything about stealing it?''

"I didn't mean…'' She shot him a swift, guilty look. "Well, yes. I guess I did. It's just that she's lived there for fifty-five years. I'd hate to hurt her.''

She hadn't helped the situation any. His frown grew positively thunderous. "Who the hell said anything about hurting her?"

"I didn't—"

"Yes, you did. You said and meant precisely that. Haven't you learned a damned thing working with me this past week? I don't steal and I don't go out of my way to hurt people, especially not little old ladies with beagle puppies named Arthur and Guinevere."

Jacq seized the topic with relief. "They were cute, weren't they? And don't you think those big floppy bows were a perfect match for those big floppy ears—"

He cut her off. "I attempt to make reasonable procurements. If there's a way to satisfy the needs of both parties, that's what I do."

"I know," Jacq apologized. "I just can't see how you're going to satisfy both parties in this case."

"I haven't figured that out, either. But give me time." He fixed her with a steady gaze. "Now do you trust me to find a way or not?"

"Of course I trust you," she said without a moment's hesitation.

Warmth lit his eyes. "Then trust this, Ms. Randell. I won't force Adele Gravis to sell until she's ready."

"I believe you."

Satisfied, he cupped the back of her head and pulled her close for a quick kiss. "That's all I needed to hear."

Snuggling into his arms again, she moistened her lips, savoring the flavor that lingered there. She couldn't believe she'd been so lucky as to find someone like Mathias—not after Elliott. She gazed at him with adoring eyes. Her black-and-white man. Her sleeping dragon. She did believe in him. Why, she could even trust him with her heart.

*   *   *

As the daylight faded, so did Jacq's optimism. With the exception of the island cabin—which they'd crossed off her list due to the lack of amenities—all the resorts the travel agency had recommended were lovely. At least, she hadn't found anything wrong with them. She just hadn't found anything right, either. After a full day of driving, not one of the places they'd inspected had been "it."

"Don't give up," Mathias said, sensing her mood. "We'll find the one."

"What if we don't? I'd feel awful if we let Patsie and Dana down. They're counting on us."

"We won't let them down. I promise."

She examined the list for the umpteenth time, nibbling on the end of her pen. "Coldwater Resort wasn't so bad. It overlooked that bay, remember?"

"The lumber company had just cut a swath of trees not ten feet from the cabin. It was depressing. Besides, 'not so bad' isn't good enough. We're looking for a place where we'd want to spend our honeymoon."

That stopped her. "Our honeymoon?"

"Yeah. *Our* honeymoon."

The set of his jaw worried her, signifying an unmistakable masculine aggressiveness. She'd noticed the trait before, but until now she'd been successful at overlooking it. "I didn't realize we were planning one," she offered lightly.

The jaw inched further out. "You're still wearing my ring, aren't you? You're still telling people we're engaged."

"That's just a game we're playing," she protested.

He turned a fierce green gaze on her, trapping her for a heated instant. "I don't play games."

She swallowed. "Our engagement was just a way to put Lynn at her ease," she tried again.

"What about Patsie and Dana? And Adele Gravis?" he demanded. "What about all the other procurements we've worked on? Or Ebbie? Were you trying to make them feel more comfortable, too?"

"No," she admitted. But his questions provoked an uncomfortable question... Why *had* she kept up the fantasy?

A smaller road branched off to the right with a large wooden sign that read, "Heaven on Earth." Mathias pulled up the gravel road and parked in front of the resort office. Shutting off the engine, he turned to look at her. "Then why continue the pretense?" he asked, echoing her own thoughts.

She couldn't tell him the truth. She wasn't even sure what that truth might be—except that wearing his ring and being with him each day had become as vital to her as breathing. "It's too soon to have this conversation," she said, switching tactics. "We've only known each other a little over a week."

"I've known you a lifetime," he said roughly. "I just didn't find you until a week ago."

With that, he climbed from the car and slammed the door behind him. Jacq sat for several stunned seconds before finding the ability to move. He'd already started toward the office, a pretty white cabin with bluish-gray shutters and two huge Christmas wreaths hooked on the walls flanking the entrance. She chased after him, breathless by the time she'd joined him on the porch.

"Do you mean that?" she demanded as he opened the front door.

His mouth tightened. "What the hell do you think?

Does it sound like a line I hand out to every woman I meet?''

"No, but—''

He spun around and grabbed her shoulders. Hauling her close, he kissed her, kissed her long and hard. She could feel his anger, his impatience. She could also feel his intense hunger and longing.

Releasing her, he said, "I am not your ex-fiancé. When I say something, I damn well mean it. You got that?''

All she could do was nod.

"Well, Merry Christmas, folks,'' an amused voice greeted them from the vicinity of the front desk.

Jacq peeked around Mathias and smiled weakly at the elderly man beaming at them from behind the counter. "Oh, hello.''

"Bobby Jacobs,'' he introduced himself. "Welcome to Heaven on Earth. Now, don't laugh at the name. My wife's something of a romantic and you'll hurt her feelings if you make fun of it.''

Jacq bit down on her lip and shook her head.

"You two want accommodations for the evening?'' he continued. "This time of year we don't keep many of our cabins open.''

"Actually—'' Jacq began.

"That would be great,'' Mathias interrupted. "We've spent the entire day on the road and we're both exhausted.''

"We're looking for honeymoon accommodations for friends of ours,'' Jacq added. "It's our wedding gift to them. Would any of your cabins be appropriate for that?''

"I've got the perfect one,'' Bobby claimed. "We had it all stocked for a couple that was due in today. But she's come down with the flu and had to cancel at the last minute. How 'bout if I let you stay there for the night? Try it out and see if you don't agree that it's the perfect spot for a honeymoon. I'll even give you a break on the price.''

"Oh, that's fantastic," she enthused. "Isn't that great, Mathias?"

He gave her a curious look, then shrugged. "If it doesn't bother you, it doesn't bother me.''

"My wife decorated the interior herself,'' Bobby continued to chat as Mathias filled out the registration card. "You've got a spectacular view of the water and trees all around. Nice and private. If you feel like cooking your own meals, there's even a kitchen. Or you can go into Port Donovan. It's walkable when the weather's nice.'' He winked. "'Course, the restaurants will deliver if you're feelin' too lazy to make your way into town.''

Thanking him for the information, Jacq and Mathias collected the key and returned to the car, following the directions they'd been given to the cabin. "What do you think?'' he asked, parking in front of the two-story A-frame.

"It's beautiful,'' she whispered, staring in awe.

The entire front was glass and offered a spectacular view of both water and woods. Walking inside, they discovered that it had been built with a reverse floor plan, the first level a giant master bedroom. In the small loft at the peak of the "A" they found a thoroughly modern kitchen as well as a dining area.

Mathias stood in front of the plate-glass windows upstairs. "It's like cooking in the treetops. I can't picture a better spot to have morning coffee.''

"This could be the one.'' Jacq hugged his arm enthusiastically. "Come on! Let's explore downstairs. Did you notice whether or not there was a fireplace?"

"You'll find it right next to the Jacuzzi and across from the king bed."

Her mouth dropped open. "You're kidding."

"Go look."

Sure enough, a raised tile dais held a Jacuzzi large enough to swim in. It was flanked on one side by the fireplace and on the other by a bank of windows. Lush ferns overflowed the sill and surrounded most of the tub.

"It must be like bathing in the middle of the forest." She could actually picture fingers of steam rising from the tub and stealing through the ferns while a fire crackled alongside.

"You'll have to give it a try."

It was tempting. Very tempting. If she were alone, she wouldn't hesitate. "I just might," she temporized.

"So are we agreed? Is this the place we want to send the Tolsons?"

Jacq nodded decisively. "This is definitely *it*. There's no point in looking any further."

"Excellent. I'll go unload the car."

As he started for the door, her gaze shifted to the king-size bed and clung there. How could she have overlooked *that*? It was then she realized precisely what she'd agreed to. Why in the world hadn't she thought of this sooner? She shot after him. "Mathias, wait!"

He turned unexpectedly, catching her as she tumbled into his arms. "Slow down, sweetheart. Where's the fire?"

"I just noticed. There's only one bed," she told the front of his shirt.

A chuckle rumbled through his chest. "How many beds did you expect the honeymoon cabin to have?"

No wonder he'd given her such a funny look when she'd suggested they spend the night here! She groaned. "I'm an idiot. I admit it, okay? But I can't... We can't..." She ground to a miserable halt.

"It's all right," he murmured, his arms tightening around her. "Everything will work out. I promise."

He knew, came the hazy realization. He knew what she'd been thinking, understood what she feared. She risked a quick look upward. "Mathias?"

"I'm not going anywhere, honey." He took a deep breath and spoke through gritted teeth. "And I won't try and seduce you tonight, if that's what's worrying you."

"Promise?"

"I promise."

He forked his hands through her hair and he kissed her just as he had in the resort office. At the first touch of his mouth, she relaxed. He wasn't like Elliott. She didn't have to worry about Mathias taking from her, deceiving her and then stealing off into the night. She trusted him. Trusted him more than she'd trusted anyone in her entire life.

Reluctantly, he released her. "Let's unpack and go explore Port Donovan. We can have dinner there and come back and relax in front of the tube."

"There's no TV," she noted.

"Oh, right." He frowned. "In that case, we'll buy a book. Several books. You brought your paints, didn't you?"

It was the first time he'd ever referred to her artwork. "Of course."

"Perfect. We'll both have something to keep us occupied."

She murmured an agreement, but thought privately that it would be interesting to see how long *that* lasted.

It lasted precisely half an hour from the moment they returned to the cabin.

Mathias jumped to his feet for the fourth time in five minutes and paced the length of the sitting room. He'd been a fool. A total idiot. How could he have imagined for one tiny second that he could spend an entire night alone with Jacq—and in a bedroom, no less—and keep his hands to himself? It was impossible. He'd been temporarily insane when he'd made that promise. A man couldn't be held responsible for his actions when he was insane, could he?

"Don't you like your book?" Jacq questioned absently as she made a small change to her sketch.

"It's fine." He glared at her downbent head. How did she do it? How did she manage to sit there looking so damned innocent while at the same time looking so damned sexy? "I'm going out for a walk," he announced abruptly.

That caught her attention. "But it's dark," she protested. "And cold."

He snagged his coat. "Cold. Good." Maybe cold would help cool him off. He opened the door and stopped dead, icy flakes slapping him in the face. Aw, hell. Cold, he welcomed. But he wasn't a total fool. Freezing cold wasn't an option. "Jacq, come look at this."

Tossing her sketch pad aside, she joined him in the doorway, staring out at the snow pelting earthward. "It's beautiful," she exclaimed, thrilled. "Do you think it'll stick? Do you think we'll get snowed in?"

He closed his eyes and groaned. Fate had a cruel sense of humor. "If we are, I'm going to need more books. A lot more books."

She linked arms with him. "Come back inside. You

can't walk in this. Why don't you start a fire and I'll check the cupboards. They must have some cocoa or coffee stashed around here somewhere.''

Reluctantly he shut the door, fighting for control. He'd be fine if she'd just stop touching him. ''Okay. But make it decaf.'' Tonight would be long enough without caffeine keeping him up half the night and adding to his edginess.

With a disgustingly cheerful smile, she headed upstairs and Mathias turned his attention to the fireplace. Not that there was much to do. It was already laid, only needing the touch of a match to start the blaze. Above him he heard Jacq opening and closing cupboard doors.

''Bobby wasn't kidding,'' she called. ''They're fully stocked. Oh! I have something you're going to appreciate.'' He heard the unmistakable tinkle of glasses just before she appeared on the circular staircase carrying two flutes and a bottle of champagne. She offered the magnum along with a smile that would have done Eve proud. ''You look like a man who could use a drink.''

Slowly he shook his head. ''There's only one thing I need. And it's not a drink.''

''Then what is it?''

She had a lot of nerve asking. His response was short and to the point. ''You.''

The stopper left the bottle with a muted pop and she jumped. But whether it was the sound that had caught her off guard or his comment, he couldn't determine. Without taking his eyes from her, he poured the champagne into the flutes. Heaven help him, she was beautiful. Firelight caressed her face, flickering across the sharp cheekbones and igniting the gold in her unique hazel-colored eyes. If he didn't find a way to break the tension, he was going to do something he'd regret—something they'd both regret.

"Sit down," he said, aware that the request sounded more like an order. "Let's talk."

"About what?" she asked warily.

He racked his brains for an innocuous subject. "Why don't we start with why you left Limelight. You never told me that particular story."

She inclined her head, kneeling on the thick wool rug in front of the fire. "Fair enough," she said, accepting the glass he handed her. "But there's not that much to tell."

"Humor me."

"Okay," she said with a shrug. "Let's see… I went to college and took business classes as Dad requested. Naturally, after graduation, I joined Limelight. Business was booming, which was great, right? Only one small problem. Much to everyone's dismay, we discovered that I was a better idea person than administrator. J.J. and Cord hadn't joined the company yet, and we needed help. So, Dad hired Elliott Drescoll."

"The fiancé?"

"Ex-fiancé," she corrected carefully. She took a sip of wine as though to rinse the sour taste of his name from her mouth. "Shortly after we hired him, he began working my accounts—with Dad's full approval, of course."

"What happened?"

"Elliott threw a huge benefit for my one remaining client—a cancer research organization. Only he deliberately made a hash of it. The organization actually lost money as a result, at a very public and embarrassing benefit. Everyone was furious and pointing fingers. In the end, we all agreed that I'd take the blame and leave the agency in an attempt to salvage what little remained of Limelight's reputation.''

''*We* decided?''

''Dad and I.''

His mouth tightened, but he didn't comment. ''And Drescoll?''

''He scooped up the bulk of Limelight's clientele and handed them over to our main competitor. He'd been free-lancing for them all along. His job had been to join our firm and turn as many clients as he could. Once he'd done that, he was paid a hefty sum by our rival and disappeared into the woodwork.''

''Where'd he go?''

''I don't know and could care less.'' She took another sip of champagne. ''He doesn't work for the competition. I do know that much. From what I gather, it was just a clever, one-shot deal.''

''He did you a favor, you realize that?''

''Yes, I do. If it hadn't been for Elliott, I'd still be a Limelighter and I'd be miserable.'' Cold anger filled her eyes. ''But that doesn't change the fact that he almost ruined my father's company and caused irreparable damage to the cancer organization we were trying to help. There's no calculating how much funding they lost or how many needy people were harmed as a result.''

''Point taken.''

She drained her glass and gestured toward him. ''Your turn. How did you decide on such an unusual occupation? I've been wondering about that ever since we met.''

''Pure chance. It started with one simple request and grew from there.''

''Someone asked you to find an item for them and it

was such a snap, you decided to turn procuring into a full-time career?''

He swirled the wine in his glass. ''I failed at that first request.''

It took her a moment to absorb what he'd said. Surprise chased across her expressive features. ''You failed?''

''Crashed and burned.''

''But I thought you told me you'd never failed to make a procurement.''

''Since I started my business, no. At the time I tried to fulfill this request I was a stockbroker.''

''I...I don't understand. Just because you blew it, you turned your whole life upside down? Changed occupations and...'' She tilted her head to one side and he watched as slowly, ever so slowly, she crept closer to the bleak center of his soul. ''And your world lost its colors.'' she whispered.

''Yeah. Something like that.'' He refilled their glasses, the hiss of bursting champagne bubbles competing with the snapping of burning logs.

''What happened? What caused the colors to fade?''

It took him a full minute to push the words past clenched teeth. He wasn't even certain he'd ever said them aloud before. ''My son died.'' He closed his eyes. ''Christopher died and so did all the colors.''

CHAPTER EIGHT

ONE minute Mathias was alone with his pain and the next strong arms were wrapped around him, easing the agony. "Christopher made the request?" Jacq questioned.

"Yes."

"And you weren't able to fulfill it?"

"No. Not that first one."

It took her a moment to catch his meaning. "But there was another? One you were able to fulfill." She didn't wait for him to respond. "Nemesis," she said, her intuitive skills amazing him.

"Yeah, Nemesis. Chris was sick a long time and we kept his bed close to the window so he could look outside. He saw a neighbor mistreating the cat and begged me to save him."

"And you did."

"It wasn't hard. A few dollars along with a few threats and the man was happy to oblige." His mouth twisted. "Of course, after failing with that first request, I'd have done anything to get my hands on that cat."

"But instead you found a way to satisfy both parties," Jacq replied evenly.

He inclined his head in acknowledgment. "Christopher and Nemesis became the best of friends. They played together, slept and ate together, were inseparable. Until..." It took him a moment to continue. "Afterward, I quit my job to try my hand at procuring. But it was too much for Lisa."

"Your wife?"

"Yes. Without Chris, nothing was the same. The marriage fell apart and we went our separate ways."

"Which left you with Nemesis, a driving determination never to fail again..." Her voice grew softer. "And a world without colors."

He lifted his head and looked at her. "That changed recently."

A tender smile touched her mouth and she smoothed her hand along the taut line of his jaw. Firelight flared within her ring. Before his eyes, awareness stirred in the emerald eyes of the dragon and the ruby heart burned with new life. For the first time in a very long time, he felt the rekindling of hope.

And it was all due to one woman.

"Mathias... Do you remember the promise you made me?" she asked.

"I've made a number of them," he observed wryly. "Which are you referring to?"

"The one not to seduce me. That one."

He grimaced. "I remember it. All too well."

"Well, to be honest..." She moistened her lips, then said in a rush, "I'd appreciate it if you'd break that promise."

Jacq watched the refusal form in Mathias's eyes, the green turning as dark and turbulent as a winter sea.

"I don't want your pity," he snapped. "When we make love—"

"—it's going to be what we both want," she finished for him. "And it is."

"Prove it."

She traced the crevices bracketing his mouth. "Did you know that when you look at me, these lines disappear?"

He started to pull from her touch, then hesitated. "So?"

"So... They disappear and in their place little bitty crow's-feet form at the corners of your eyes. Care to guess why?"

He shook his head, tension lending his jaw a rock-hard set. "I haven't the faintest idea."

"It's because when I'm with you, you laugh," she said softly. "I've noticed other things, too."

"What?" The word seemed dragged from him.

"Your eyes turn color when I walk into the room."

That snagged his interest. "So do yours."

She caught her breath in delight. "Do they really? What color do they turn?"

"It's not one color, but a bunch of them. The gold gets brighter and there's this misty gray that shows up."

"Yours go a deep, dark green." Her brow furrowed. "I haven't quite got the exact shade worked out. But I will. It's sort of a hungry green."

A laugh broke from him. "Hungry?"

"Yeah. Hungry and determined and lustful."

His amusement faded. "I think we can both agree that I want you. Badly. I have from the first moment I saw you."

"Really?" She shivered, wishing he'd stop being so darned stubborn and kiss her.

"There's never been any question of that. But you still haven't proven the reverse is true."

"That's only because you haven't been looking." She captured his hand and cupped it to her breast. The nipple surged against his palm. "Do you feel it?" she whispered. "Is that proof enough for you? I want you so bad it actually hurts."

For a long minute the only sound in the room was the

ragged give and take of his breath. "Don't do this, Jacq," he demanded hoarsely. "Because I won't be able to stop if you keep pushing. It's been too long and I need you too much to be honorable."

"Honorable won't get me in your bed. And that's precisely where I'd like to be. This isn't pity, Mathias. Can't you tell the difference?"

"Not at this particular moment." He closed his eyes. "I have to think. I need to consider—"

"You don't have to consider anything but this."

She crept more fully into his arms, wrapping herself around him. He felt taut and powerful against her, a sharp contrast to her softer, more pliant curves. Their scents mingled, his as intensely masculine as hers was delicately feminine. He seemed to drink in the sweetness. His hands moved on her, shaping the swell of her breast before catching the swollen peak between his fingers. She rocked her hips against his.

He groaned harshly in response. "Honey, don't do that. You're killing me."

"I can't stop. I don't want to stop. You asked for proof? Well, here it is. This is desire." She caught the lobe of his ear between her teeth and tugged. "Real. Honest. Passionate. Desire."

He surged to his feet, bringing her with him. "I hope to hell you know what you're doing."

Oh, she knew, all right. She was finally giving herself to the man she loved with all her heart and soul.

He carried her to the king-size bed, releasing her only long enough to sweep back the covers. She sensed the desperate urgency he could barely contain, the battle he waged to be gentle.

"Clothes," he muttered. "We're still wearing clothes."

"They come off," she soothed.

She helped him work the buttons and zips, aware that if she didn't, he'd resort to ripping them from their bodies. A wildfire burned in his gaze, his face a mask of desperation. Her clothing disappeared first and he couldn't stop touching her—the sensitive nipples crowning her breasts, then the silken skin of her abdomen, and finally the nest of curls at the juncture of her thighs. He was intent on charting it all. All too soon an unmistakable urgency overrode his desire to explore. His shirt hit the floor, followed by his pants and shorts.

Jacq gazed in wonder. She'd always considered Mathias the most impressive man she'd ever met. But that was before she'd seen him nude. He truly was a dragon—fierce and untamed and powerful.

"You're beautiful. So incredibly beautiful," she told him. Her hands collided with the abrasive black hair of his chest and she traced the tough sinewy lines beneath, delighted by the well-formed muscles.

"Lower," he demanded.

She did as he ordered, following the arrow of hair to its source. He groaned at the first tentative touch, shuddering, every muscle drawn taut. He tried to say something, but only a guttural groan escaped his throat. Finally, he shook his head and palmed the sides of her face. He kissed her, again and again and again—her eyes, her cheeks, her chin and throat and then, at long last, her mouth. His tongue drove inward, hot and urgent and demanding. She couldn't get enough of him, her hunger spiraling to match his.

The bed rose up to meet them and she clasped her hands around his neck, reveling in the delicious press of his weight. She wanted him. Now. "Please, Mathias. Don't make me wait any longer."

For a brief instant he hesitated. "Tell me this isn't for Chris. I have to know before we take this any further."

It wasn't. But it did give her pause. "Mathias, listen—"

"I'm not sure I can." He buried his face in the curve of her shoulder, his breath hot against her throat. "Don't tell me it's pity. Anything but that."

"It's not pity. I promise." She held him close, fighting the urge to say to hell with everything but attaining the gratification Mathias offered. "Just listen to me for a minute. I'm not ready to start on the first of those four children," she said frankly. "And I don't think you are, either."

He lifted his head to look at her, his eyes black with unfulfilled passion. "An hour ago, I would have agreed with you. Now I'm not so sure." Meeting her serious gaze, he smoothed the curls from her face. "Don't worry, sweetheart. I'll take care of it. I have no intention of bringing a child into this world until it's what we both want."

It was all she needed to hear.

Tenderly, he found her mouth again and their passion became a dance, a fluid ballet of movement. He made love to her with every word and touch and kiss. And when he finally parted her legs and fit himself against her warmth, it felt as natural and undeniable as life itself.

What came next was ancient and timeless and perfect. It was the meeting and joining of souls, the most profound of all unions. It left an indelible impression Jacq would carry forever after. And in her heart, she knew Mathias would, too.

For in that timeless moment, they became one.

Mathias awoke to a familiar blackness. It was early. Or late. He couldn't be certain which. Only one thing mattered. Jacq lay secure within the haven of his arms. Her curls caressed his face and he closed his eyes, savoring the sensation. He didn't know how it happened, or why he'd been so gifted.

But at some point during the night this woman had returned color to his world.

Just as dawn crept through the windows, Jacq flipped her sketchbook closed and returned to bed. She snuggling into Mathias's waiting arms and smiled in drowsy satisfaction. Finally. Finally it had happened.

At some point during the night, her sleeping dragon had awoken.

Much to Bobby Jacobs's delight, Jacq and Mathias stayed at the resort for two more nights. If the proprietor found their excuse about not wanting to chance the snow-slick streets a trifle thin, he hid it well. But the unvarnished truth was, they couldn't bear to leave Heaven on Earth.

Early Monday morning Jacq reluctantly returned to her cottage. She listened patiently while Angel scolded her for being gone so long. Apparently it didn't matter that Jacq had arranged for a friend to stop by for a twice-daily feed-and-play session. After taking the time to soothe Angelica's hurt feelings, Jacq played back the single message on her recorder. It was from her father.

"Where are you?" he demanded. "We need you. It's serious."

With a sigh she retrieved her coat. Opening the front door she found her sister standing on the porch, her fist poised to knock. Jacq blinked in surprise. "Oh! Hello."

"I'm glad I found you before Dad," J.J. said in greeting. And for the first time in over three years, she walked in without requesting permission.

"What's happened?" Jacq asked in alarm. "You look terrible."

"Gee, thanks." J.J. stopped in the middle of the living room and eyed the overnight bag sitting there. She gestured toward it with the magazine she held rolled in her hand. "Where did you go? We've been trying to reach you for three whole days."

"I was with Mathias. That should make you happy. Right?"

J.J. turned, her expression tight with anger. "It doesn't make me happy in the least. Not after what he's done."

"Uh-oh. I assume that means the meeting with King Investments didn't go well," Jacq guessed.

"Now there's the understatement of the century."

Jacq held up her hands. "I warned you I couldn't help with this. You're on your own," she stated firmly. And then she ruined it by asking, "Is the client really that bad?"

"Maybe you'd better ask who the client is," J.J. suggested.

Despite the central heating, Jacq felt cold. Ice cold. She sank into the nearest chair, clutching her coat more tightly and wishing with all her heart that it was Mathias's instead of her own. "It's Elliott, isn't it?" she whispered.

"Yes," her sister confirmed with a ragged sigh. "It's Elliott. He goes by the name Eddie Drysart now. But it's still him."

Jacq shook her head. "I can't help you. I just can't."

"You may not have any choice."

"*Why*?"

J.J. unrolled the business magazine she held and offered it to Jacq. "Page forty, under the entertainment section."

Jacq flipped to the page and froze. There she found a photo of one of her paintings. "Jack Rabbitt—the author and illustrator whose identity remains shrouded in secrecy—now ranks number one with children worldwide," the article stated.

But it was the painting they'd chosen to run alongside the article that proved the most damning. It was one of her favorite, portraying a fairy riding a butterfly. The wings of the butterfly swept upward, concealing the fairy from the shoulders down. But sunlight turned the wings to gossamer, revealing the fairy's silhouette through a swirl of soft color.

Of course, the identity of the fairy was unmistakable.

"It's me," J.J. said. "Which means that you're the mysterious Jack Rabbitt."

Denials were pointless. "Has Dad seen this?"

"He's the one who showed me. We... We went out and bought all of your books. Good grief, Jacq!" she blurted. "They're beautiful. Why didn't you tell us what you were doing?"

"Do you really need to ask? After that fiasco with Elliott, I needed my privacy. I was desperate for anonymity. And Limelighters aren't exactly renowned for their discretion."

J.J. nodded. "That's true enough." She slanted her sister a humor-filled glance. "I can't believe you turned Cord into a troll, though."

Jacq grinned. "Don't knock it. He's one of my most popular characters."

"And you made Dad a king?"

"Fitting, don't you think?"

"He's so proud, I think he might pop." J.J.'s expression turned self-conscious. "And the fairy? Why did you choose that for me?"

"Symbolic. I keep hoping one day you'll break free and fly on your own."

"She's lovely."

"And naked," Jacq teased.

J.J. blushed. "Well… Fortunately, it *is* a children's book. You've been very clever at concealing her, ah—"

"Assets?" They broke into laughter and Jacq realized it had been a long time since she'd enjoyed such a light-hearted moment with her sister. "So I assume Dad's looking for a way to use my identity to Limelight's advantage. Or to force my hand so I'll help with Elliott."

Pain robbed the amusement from J.J.'s eyes. "I guess we deserve that," she said softly. "But you're wrong."

"He doesn't want Jack Rabbitt to save Limelight?" Jacq questioned in surprise.

"It isn't Dad who wants to use you."

"I don't understand. Who—" Jacq caught her breath in horror. "*Elliott*?"

J.J. nodded. "You should have seen Dad. As soon as he found out who owned King Investments, he gave Elliott hell and started to walk out. But then Elliott gave Dad the magazine and threatened to reveal your identity to the press."

"It doesn't matter! Limelight can't work with that—"

"It gets worse, Jacq. Elliott threatened to dredge up all those lies that were spread about you after the cancer benefit fiasco. He was horrible! Arrogant. Hateful. So sure of himself. He said no one would ever buy your books again once they found out who you really were and what you'd done all those years ago."

"What did Dad do?" Jacq asked numbly.

"Oh, Jacq, you would have been so proud of him. He

repeated your words almost verbatim. He very calmly said that sometimes the only right answer is a flat-out no. Then he told Elliott to go to hell and walked out.''

Tears gathered in Jacq's eyes. "Good for him. I wish I'd been there to see it.''

J.J. glanced hesitantly at her sister. "Dad went to see Blackstone first thing this morning to explain our decision.''

Jacq stared in alarm. "But Mathias doesn't know who I am.''

"Don't worry. Dad won't spill the beans about that. He just wants to set the record straight about Elliott and tell Blackstone that Limelight International doesn't work for scum like Drescoll no matter what the financial incentive.''

"Mathias doesn't, either,'' Jacq instantly leaped to his defense. "I guarantee he didn't know about Elliott or he'd never have taken him on as a client.''

"That still doesn't solve the basic problem, though, does it?''

Jacq caught her lower lip between her teeth and shook her head. No. It didn't. If she didn't come up with a solution—and fast—she'd have her life destroyed all over again by Elliott. And she refused to allow that to happen. She jumped to her feet and grabbed the phone with only one thought in mind.

She had to speak to Mathias. He'd know what to do.

Jacq arrived at Mathias's office on the dot of twelve for their lunch appointment. To her surprise, Ebbie wasn't around. Neither was Mathias. Amazing. She couldn't remember his ever being late before. With a shrug, she closeted herself inside his office. At least she'd have an opportunity to add to her painting while she waited for him.

She dropped her satchel on the chair by his desk, amused to discover only one file cluttering the glass surface; he was fast running out of room for even that. She started to move the folder when the label caught her eye. "Christmas procurements," it read. Curiosity got the better of her and after a guilty glance toward the door, she flipped it open and scanned the contents. Ebbie had stapled a newspaper article to the inside cover and after reading it, Jacq shook her head.

"Oh, no, he says. I'm not playing Santa Claus. Ha!"

The article described a "mystery man" who donated his expertise for the month of December in order to grant a few deserving individuals their Christmas wish. Various requests filled the folder. She found a profile on Dana and Patsie. And the Davenports. And a whole slew of other familiar names. She saw Operation Toys in there, as well. She'd been actively helping with that one—calling on neighborhood businesses for toy donations that were then distributed to local shelters for the homeless and abused.

She closed the file with a smile. If someone had told her that one day she'd fall in love with Santa Claus, she'd have laughed in their face. Well, it would seem the laugh was on her, because that was precisely what she'd done.

Setting the file carefully to one side, she opened her satchel and began removing paints and brushes. Knowing Mathias needed the information about Lynn in order to fulfill some sort of Christmas wish, put a whole new light on the matter. She'd definitely have to reconsider how to handle that situation.

Bending over the desk, she quickly became engrossed

in her work, losing all track of time until the office door slammed closed. She jumped, knocking over a tiny vial of paint. Metallic yellow bled across the glass. Prepared to scold the offender for being so careless, she looked up and froze.

"Elliott." His name left in a breathless rush.

"Well, well," he murmured, leaning against the black double doors. "How convenient. The cause of all my troubles sitting here waiting for me."

"I'm not waiting for you. Mathias—"

"Isn't around," he cut in, advancing toward her. "But you are. Which gives me the opportunity to thank you personally for lousing up my latest little scam."

"What are you talking about? What scam?"

"My investment company scam. I had it all figured out, you know."

She moistened her lips, desperate to keep him talking until she could think of a way to escape. "Why don't you tell me about it?"

A humorless smile swept across his well-shaped lips, letting her know he wasn't fooled in the least by her question. "You can't delay the inevitable. I will make you pay for what you've done."

"At least satisfy my curiosity first." She prayed an appeal to his vanity would work as well now as it always had in the past. "What clever scheme did you come up with this time?"

To her intense relief, he took the bait. "I had it all figured. Approach Mathias Blackstone, the man with the impeccable reputation. Make my request intriguing enough so he'd take me on. Have him 'procure' the perfect location, the perfect clientele and the perfect publicity for King Investments. And then fleece as many investors as possible before retiring to a tropical island."

Fury darkened his expression. "The only thing I hadn't anticipated was Blackstone turning the job over to Limelight."

"It must have come as a nasty shock," she couldn't resist taunting.

She instantly regretted the crack, realizing it only served to feed his anger. "Very," he agreed, taking another threatening step toward the desk. "I almost took off then."

"What stopped you?"

"I came across the article on Jack Rabbitt. You really shouldn't have used your sister for a model," he chided. "It was a dead giveaway. That's when I realized I could blackmail your father into keeping quiet. And it would have worked, too, if you hadn't interfered."

She leaped to her feet, relieved to have the full width of Mathias's desk between them. "I didn't interfere. I didn't even know who the owner of King Investments was until this morning."

"But you told Blackstone my real identity and that's all that matters. He made it clear we wouldn't be doing business together now or ever. And I have you to thank for that." He fixed her with cold blue eyes and she wondered how she could have ever thought him attractive. "Of course, you'll soon regret sticking your nose where it doesn't belong. Once the buying public discovers your identity, your career will be over."

She said the first thing that came into her head. "Mathias will stop you. If you do anything to hurt me, he'll make sure you pay."

Elliott lifted an eyebrow. "And why would he do that?"

She opened her mouth to respond. But as it turned out, she didn't have to say a word. He reached the desk, glanced casually at what she'd been painting and swore viciously. Before she realized what he intended, he rounded the desk and grabbed her arm, shaking her.

"What are you to him? Answer me!"

"We're engaged! See?" She held up a trembling hand and showed him the ring. Emerald dragon's eyes flashed a grim warning. "Now let go of me."

It was clear he hadn't known of their involvement. It was equally clear the news unsettled him. Before he had a chance to consider his next move, the door crashed open and Jacq fought to free herself as a fire-breathing dragon shot across the room toward them. It was over in the blink of an eye. Elliott lay on the floor, cupping his nose and Mathias stood over him, still breathing fire.

"My nob!" Elliott moaned. "You bwoke it!"

"Is that all?" Mathias curled his hands into fists. "Then I suggest you get out before I decide to break something more vital."

Elliott scrambled backward across the floor. "You'll pay!" he shouted. "I'll make you both pay."

Mathias reached down, grabbed Elliott by the tie and yanked him to his feet. "Listen up Drysart or Drescoll or whatever the hell you call yourself. I've made a few phone calls about you. I've even had a conversation with several very angry law enforcement officials. For some reason, they're real keen to get their hands on you. Now why is that, do you suppose?"

Elliott turned white and moaned pitifully.

"I see you understand the situation. You do or say anything to cause harm to Jacq or her family—if so much as a single whisper comes to my ears, you'll wish you'd never been born. Are we clear?"

"Give me a head start," Elliott pleaded. "I swear I

won't do anything, just give me a day to get out of town.''

''You better have that rock you're gonna crawl under all picked out. Because you have exactly one hour before I make that phone call.'' Mathias tossed Elliott toward the door. ''Now get out of here.''

The instant he'd left, Jacq threw herself into a pair of waiting arms. ''Oh, Mathias!'' she exclaimed tearfully. ''How could you?''

He looked thunderstruck. ''You didn't want me to hit him?''

''Of course I did. I meant how could you have broken rule number two? You said you'd always be where you said, when you said. And you weren't.''

He groaned. ''I'm so sorry, sweetheart. Are you all right? Did he hurt you?''

She nodded against his chest, barely stifling a sob. ''Yes, he did.''

''Where? Where are you hurt?'' He pushed her back, his gaze sweeping over her with unmistakable urgency. ''What did he do?''

''He ruined my painting!'' she informed him in tragic tones. ''Just look.''

Together they studied his desk. A huge black dragon lay sprawled in the very center, luminescent green eyes glaring warily at the world. Beneath one paw he'd trapped a nasty little rat that bore an uncanny resemblance to Elliott. And curled up at his side was another dragon, a rather feminine golden-brown dragon with laughing hazel eyes.

''What did he do?'' Mathias asked in confusion. ''It seems fine to me. Although if he saw that rat, I can understand why he lost his temper.''

''He made me smear the yellow all over—'' She

blinked, doing a quick double take. Yellow paint arrowed down from one corner and ended just at the top of the male dragon. It gave her an idea. A wonderful, exciting, delicious idea. "Never mind. You're right. It's perfect."

"I'm glad you—"

"Oh! By the way... This belongs to you." She picked up the file of Christmas procurements and held it out. "And before you ask, yes I looked."

He took the file and tossed it to one side. "Did you?"

"Yes. You know something else?" She threw her arms around him again, planting a quick kiss at the corner of his mouth. "I adore you."

"How much of the file did you read?" he asked in an expressionless voice.

"Just the article in front. Then I saw a page for Dana and Patsie. I also recognized Lynn's name as well as a few others."

"That's it?"

"I think so." She pulled back. "Why?"

"Those files are private, Jacq. I didn't want you to know about the Christmas wishes because—"

She gazed up at him with shining eyes. "Because I might think you're wonderful?"

"Because they're confidential. Sometimes they don't work out."

"I'm sorry. I'll be more careful in the future." She tipped her head to one side. "Am I forgiven?"

He closed his eyes. "It's me who's sorry, Jacq. I didn't mean to snap. I just have one procurement I'm working on that's proving more difficult than I'd anticipated."

"Is it anything I can help with?" she asked solicitously.

"Not yet. Maybe later on." He glanced at his watch. "Look. I have a client arriving any minute now. Could we get together tonight instead of for lunch?"

"I'd love to." Her brows drew together. "Are you positive you're all right?"

"You want proof?" Not waiting for an answer, he drew her into his arms and kissed her. It was a kiss that stirred memories of the weekend. Of bubble baths in the Jacuzzi and making love by a roaring fire. Of sitting quietly drinking coffee and sharing confidences. Of dawn's first light glistening on snowflakes as they tumbled from a wintry sky. And of peaceful sunsets over the water. "Does that reassure you?" he murmured.

"Mmm. Perfect." Reluctantly she left the haven of his arms and returned her paints and brushes to her satchel. "Would you like to come to the cottage for dinner? I could burn something for you."

He laughed. "Now how can I refuse an offer like that?"

She wrinkled her nose at him. "Most people find it amazingly easy."

"Well, not me. I'll be there at six. And I promise not to break rule number two again."

"I'm holding you to that," she warned and, giving him one last kiss, she left the office.

As she waited for the elevator, Jacq considered the finishing touches she'd put on the desk. For the first time in her life, she had something to thank Elliott for. If it hadn't been for him... The elevator doors opened and a woman stepped out.

"Lynn!" Jacq exclaimed in delight. "How great to—"

The woman cast her a bewildered look, clinging

tightly to the man at her side. "I'm sorry," she said. "My name's Shawna Carter. Do I...do I know you?"

It took Jacq a full thirty seconds to gather her wits sufficiently to respond. "No, no. I'm sorry. I thought you were someone else. You look so much like her." She smiled weakly. Only younger. And pregnant.

Tears gathered in soft blue eyes identical to Lynn's. "Do I? Look like her, I mean."

"Yeah, you do."

The man at Shawna's side stirred. "Come on, love. We're going to be late for our appointment."

"Nice talking to you," Jacq murmured.

Shawna nodded and allowed her husband to draw her along the hallway to Mathias's door. Jacq watched them go.

So Lynn had a daughter. A sweet, beautiful daughter. No question, this had to be Mathias's Christmas procurement. Which gave Jacq an idea. Maybe, just maybe she could help him grant this particular wish.

CHAPTER NINE

"I KNOW you don't understand," Jacq said patiently. She glanced over her shoulder and lowered her voice. "Listen, I'm with Lynn now. Can you get Shawna over to Sunset Hill Park at one? It's up on the bluff overlooking Shilshole Bay. Do you know where I mean?"

"I'm familiar with the area," Mathias replied. "But what excuse am I supposed to use?"

"You're inventive. Come up with something. I've got a plan that just might work. All you have to do is be at Sunset Hill Park by one. Choose a bench and plant yourself there, okay?"

"Jacq—"

She winced at the warning tone. "Relax. I can handle this. All you have to do is bring Shawna."

"You're not even supposed to know about Shawna. Now you're going to procure a mother for her?"

"It isn't my fault that I ran into her outside of your office," she retorted, stung. "Or that I put two and two together. Since I did, you might as well let me do what I can to help. All I need from you is a little cooperation."

"If this goes wrong..."

"You can blame me. Look, no one else will be aware of what's happening. If it works, I'll wave and you bring Shawna over. Otherwise, I'll shake my head and you cut out."

"How will I know it's what Lynn wants?"

"You won't. But I will." She released an exasperated sigh. "You'll have to trust me, Mathias."

"Dammit, Jacq!"

"I know. Love's hell. Will you do it?"

"Trust you? Absolutely."

She felt oddly humbled by his response. "Thanks," she said. "That means a lot. But what I meant was, will you bring Shawna to the park?"

"We'll be there. And, Jacq?"

"What?"

"I..." He sighed. "Be careful."

Jacq stifled a laugh. For a man so crazy in love, he sure had a difficult time saying the words. "I love you, too. 'Bye."

She hung up before he had a chance to respond. He'd say it. Soon. Once he sat down and analyzed every aspect, explored every option and alternative, he'd tell her how he felt in no uncertain terms. Until then she refused to try and force a declaration from him.

"Is everything all right?" Lynn asked curiously, joining her by the bank of pay phones. "Mathias didn't mind you breaking your lunch date?"

"He takes my whims surprisingly well. In fact, he's broken the rules more often than I have." It gave her a great deal of satisfaction to say that.

Lynn's eyes widened. "Rules?"

"Didn't I tell you about them?" Jacq linked arms with her newfound friend. "This should give you a chuckle...."

The rest of the morning passed in a pleasant frenzy of last-minute Christmas shopping. Finally, exhausted, the two loaded packages into the trunk of Jacq's tiny compact.

"I don't know what Mel will say when he sees all the things I bought," Lynn fussed.

"Well, I do," Jacq replied. "He'll roll his eyes in pretended exasperation, mutter something only a man would say about women and shopping. And then he'll decide he should run out and get you just one more stocking stuffer."

Lynn laughed in delight. "You're right. That's precisely what he'll do."

"I'm starved," Jacq mentioned casually. "How about stopping for lunch?"

"I hoped you'd say that. I know this fantastic deli. Their sandwiches are out of this world."

"Sounds great. And I know an even more fantastic spot to eat them. If you don't mind braving the cold, we can enjoy the December sunshine while it lasts and at the same time watch some boats go by."

Lynn shrugged. "I'm game if you are."

Shortly after one, they were parked on a bench overlooking Shilshole Bay and Puget Sound and staring at the white-tipped Olympic Mountains. It was a view guaranteed to appease even the most tortured soul.

Jacq glanced over her shoulder and saw Mathias climb from an unfamiliar car. Shawna and her husband were with him. As the three walked to the wire fence to take in the view, Jacq fought to control an unexpected and severe case of butterflies. This was the right thing to do. She'd never been more certain of anything. Still, she crossed her fingers, praying she wasn't about to make the biggest mistake of her life.

"Lynn... Would you mind if I ask a personal question?"

Relaxed and intent on the view, Lynn shrugged. "Not at all. Ask away."

"I know this is going to sound odd—"

"Something you have to say is going to sound odd?" Lynn teased. "Don't be ridiculous."

Jacq flashed a quick grin. "I guess when you put it like that…"

"I'm kidding. Go ahead. Ask anything you'd like."

"The thing is…" Jacq took a deep breath and plunged in. "I recently discovered that I've been working for Santa Claus."

Lynn blinked in amazement. "Come again?"

"To be honest, it surprised the hell out of me, too." Jacq turned to face her friend, resting a bent elbow on the back of the bench and cupping her chin in her palm. "I always thought Santa was this jolly fat man with a white beard and a red suit. But he's not."

"He isn't?" Lynn asked in confusion.

"No. He's actually quite beautiful. And sexy. Very sexy."

"Jacq? Are you feeling okay? Do you want me to call someone?"

"I'm fine. Honest." She frowned. "To get back to Santa Claus… I just found out something rather wonderful. You see, he has the most amazing ability to grant wishes." She paused to consider. "I suppose he could be an angel. Although, even I'm forced to admit he has a few too many faults for that. So, I guess we'd better stick with the Santa Claus theory."

Lynn gave an incredulous laugh. "You can't be serious!"

"I'm very serious," Jacq replied calmly. "And I was thinking…. Since this guy's running around granting all these Christmas wishes, why don't I try and get him to grant one for you."

Lynn fought to keep a straight face. "Well, that's very nice of you, but I already have everything I need."

Jacq shook her head. "I'm not talking about something you *need*. I'm talking about something you want with all your heart." She gave Lynn a moment to absorb her comment, then said, "Just think. If you could have any wish fulfilled, no matter how impossible, what would it be?"

Lynn gave a bewildered shrug. "Okay. I'll play along. One wish, right?"

"Yep. Anything you want."

"I don't know. How about a million dollars?"

"They aren't those sorts of wishes," Jacq explained. "They're more personal."

"Oh. Then you already know the answer. I'd wish Mel and I could have had children." Lynn's smile turned bittersweet. "Somehow I don't think your Santa can grant that wish, can he?"

"No, I'm afraid not. And since that isn't possible?" Jacq prompted gently. "What else would you choose?"

"Then I'd wish..." Her brows drew together as she deliberated. "I'd wish for the next best thing."

"Which is?"

"I'd wish—" Lynn drew a shaky breath, tears unexpectedly filling her eyes. "Oh, Jacq. Why are you doing this?"

"Because you're my friend and I want to make you happy."

Lynn bowed her head, the words torn from her. "I'd wish I could have known my—" She covered her face with her hands, clearly unable to go on.

"You'd wish you could have known your daughter?" Jacq finished softly.

Slowly, Lynn lowered her hands, every scrap of color draining from her face. "What did you say?"

"If that's not your wish, I can tell Santa I was wrong," Jacq began in alarm.

"No, it's my wish!" Her voice broke. "It really is my wish! It is!"

"In that case..." Slowly, Jacq shifted on the bench so Lynn could see past her to where Mathias stood with Shawna. "Her name is Shawna Carter. And her one Christmas wish in all the world is to meet her mother. I hoped it would be your Christmas wish, as well."

Lynn lifted shaking hands to her mouth, tears rolling freely down her cheeks. "My daughter," she half moaned. "My daughter."

As though sensing something odd, Shawna's head jerked up. Slowly, she turned in their direction, locking gazes with her mother. Fear and hope were written in equal measures on her youthful face. Lynn stood, walking tentatively in Shawna's direction. And then they were both running, meeting halfway and throwing their arms around each other, talking in frantic gasps. At one point they pulled apart and Lynn touched Shawna's rounded stomach with a gentle hand. And then they were hugging again.

Jacq sat, unable to move, surprised to discover that her own face was wet with tears. Thank heaven it had worked out. Oh, thank heaven.

"You did good, sweetheart," Mathias murmured from behind.

She'd been so focused on Lynn and Shawna, Jacq hadn't even noticed his approach. She flew off the bench and into his arms. "I was so scared," she confessed tearfully. "I started to worry about what would happen if I was wrong. Maybe I should have taken more time, talked to Lynn some more. Maybe I was being too impulsive.''

"You did fine,'' he soothed. "Turn around and look.''

She did as he directed. The two women had moved to a nearby bench where they sat, their heads close together. Shawna's husband stood beside them, beaming in relief.

"I never stopped to consider,'' Jacq murmured. "Lynn couldn't have been more than just a baby when she gave birth.''

"Sixteen. Five years younger than Shawna is now.''

"It must have been incredibly difficult to put her child up for adoption.'' She turned a questioning gaze on Mathias. "And Shawna? What made her come looking for Lynn?''

"I think her pregnancy prompted the search.''

"Shawna's adoptive parents don't object?''

"Her mother died when she was eight. Her father passed away just recently. But even if they'd lived, they wouldn't have objected. Shawna had a wonderful relationship with them both.''

"And now Shawna has a grandmother for her baby,'' Jacq commented softly. "And if she'll allow it, a mother for herself. Lucky girl. She's going to adore Lynn.''

"And Mel, too, I hope.'' Mathias glanced over his shoulder. "Here he is now. Right on time.''

"You called him?'' Jacq asked in surprise.

"I figured no matter how this turned out, Lynn would want him here.''

"How did he take the news?''

"Don't look so nervous,'' Mathias reassured. "He's always known about the baby Lynn gave up.''

"Does he... Does he mind that Shawna's decided to approach Lynn after all these years?''

"He's thrilled—for his wife's sake as well as his own. When we spoke he said he'd always wanted a daughter and with a grandchild on the way it would be a double blessing."

Mel lifted a hand in greeting, clearly torn between the urge to be polite and the overwhelming desire to get to his wife. Mathias waved him off and with a look of relief, Mel joined Lynn and Shawna.

Jacq heaved a sigh. "I want to stay and watch, but we shouldn't intrude. They need time alone." She caught Mathias by the hand. "Come on, Santa. Our work here is through. Let's climb into your sleigh and head back to the North Pole."

"I'd love to. There's only one problem."

She smiled. "Reindeers on strike?"

"Nope. My sleigh has a broken runner."

"Okay. We'll use my Ford." She cast him a teasing glance. "But you'd better get that runner fixed and quick. Otherwise you're going to look pretty silly landing on roofs in my compact."

He flicked the tip of her nose. "Not as silly as you'll look, pulling it, Rudolph."

"Is my nose red?" she asked self-consciously.

"A delightful shade of pink."

"That happens whenever I cry." She cast a wistful glance toward Lynn and Shawna. "I just can't help it. I'm sentimental."

"I'm glad you are." Mathias gave her a lingering kiss. "Very glad."

"You've *what*?"

"Now, Mathias," Jacq began nervously. "You told me to make the arrangements for Operation Toys and I did."

"Making the arrangements means delivering the toys to the various shelters and homes. It does not mean filling my office building with a hundred screaming kids. Nor does it mean putting up a twenty-foot tree. And it especially doesn't mean decorating this place so it looks like—" He glanced around, glaring.

"So it looks like Christmas?" she offered mildly.

"Yes! No. Dammit, Jacq! And what's this?" He indicated the huge box she'd put on his chair.

"A Santa suit. It's for when you hand out the presents."

He jerked back as though it might bite him. "Oh, no. I'm not wearing that Santa suit and I'm certainly not handing out any presents."

"Why not?" she demanded. "Do you have something better to do with your time?"

"Yes! No. Dammit, Jacq!"

She planted her hands on her hips. "It's easy to simply throw money at a problem and hope it goes away."

"I don't do that," he retorted, stung.

"Normally, that's true. But in this case, that seems to be precisely what you're doing. Come on, Mathias," she wheedled. "It's just one day out of your life. And it's for a good cause. Besides, they're—"

She stopped abruptly, realizing what she'd been about to say, realizing too why he was so desperate to wriggle out of the arrangements she'd made.

He sighed in defeat. "They're children."

"Oh, Mathias." She wrapped her arms around his waist. "I'm sorry. I didn't think."

He rested his chin on the top of her head, her curls tickling his chin and mouth. "No, you're right. It is only one day. I'll hand out the presents. But I'm *not* wearing the suit. And that's final."

"You don't have to," she soothed. "The kids can do without a Santa this year."

He winced. "All right. You win. I'll wear the damned suit. But those kids are absolutely, positively, not allowed to sit on my knee. I have to draw the line somewhere."

She snuggled deeper into his embrace. "Whatever you think best. I'm sure they'll understand about the knee thing. And if they don't, you can explain it to them."

He sighed. "I'm not going to win this fight, am I?"

She looked up in surprise. "Did you think you would?"

The smile he gave her came with astonishing ease. "I think I'd have been disappointed if I had."

The day of the Christmas party proved an unqualified success. Jacq tried to hide her nervousness from Mathias as the event initially got rolling. She couldn't help worrying about how he'd handle having an office building full of children. But her fears were swiftly alleviated. After an initial hesitation, he jumped right into the thick of things.

Soon she found him organizing the decorating of the Christmas tree, busily lifting one child after another so they could hang their ornaments. Not long after that he manned the food table, distributing punch and cookies. And later still she caught him playing a fierce game of freeze tag. Toward the end of the day, he donned the Santa suit and handed out toys. The instant everyone had a gift, he got down on the floor and played.

Silently she thanked her lucky stars that once again her impulsiveness hadn't caused any harm.

At dusk, the party began to break up and before long

the last sleepy child reluctantly departed. The resulting silence was deafening.

"It looks like we were hit by a tornado," Jacq said, and then groaned. "Oh, no! I just realized something."

Mathias leaned against the nearest wall and slowly sank to the floor. At some point he'd discarded his red velvet jacket, fake beard and padding. Only his Santa cap remained. But it had slipped to one side so it sat cocked low over one red-rimmed eye. "What did you just realize?" he asked with a huge yawn.

She slid to the floor beside him and drew her knees to her chest. "I didn't arrange for a cleanup crew to come and take care of this mess."

He grinned smugly. "Fortunately, I did."

That perked her up for an instant. "Really?"

"Santa never lies," he informed her gravely.

Jacq lowered her head to his lap. "Does Santa sleep?" she mumbled.

He tilted his head back against the wall. "Oh, yeah. Santa definitely does that."

Jacq had no idea what time she finally awoke. Late, past midnight, she guessed, and the building had taken on an eerie silence. Mathias continued to sleep but she was suddenly wide awake and possessed by a truly brilliant idea. One or two of the toys they'd collected from various neighborhood businesses had been confiscated because they were inappropriate for young children. Ebbie had hidden them away in a storage closet and Jacq intended to make use of them. Right now.

Sneaking into the closet she removed two huge plastic slingshots and the "balls" that went with them—each of which contained a different colored glow-in-the-dark powder. She crept back to where Mathias slept and gently placed one of the slingshots and a bag of ammunition in his lap. Then she tiptoed through the building, switching off most of the lights.

Rejoining Mathias, she hesitated. As much as she wanted to sneak up and pelt him with one of the powdered balls, she decided it would be too cruel to wake him in such a manner. So instead she aimed for the wall over his head. Powder splattered a foot above him and rained down in a bright yellow cloud. It was then she realized she'd made a serious tactical error.

Mathias wasn't asleep.

Before she could stop laughing long enough to reload, he fired off a series of shots. It turned out he had impeccable aim. Orange, indigo and pink powder smoked her arms and stomach. With a screech of dismay, she took off running. For half an hour, they stalked each other through the darkened building. If it hadn't been for the glow-in-the-dark powder, she doubted they'd have ever found each other. Finally, only two balls remained and she decided to make them count. She snuck toward Mathias's office, certain the ever-methodical Mr. Blackstone would soon track her down. Crouching behind the door just inside his office, she waited.

It didn't take long. Five minutes later, the door cautiously swung open and he eased into the room. She wouldn't get a better opportunity. Jumping up, she shot him square in the back. The powder bullet exploded on impact, leaving a beautiful ring of glow-in-the-dark green on his shirt.

He whirled and ducked just as she got off her final round. It whizzed over his head and landed with a splat on a stack of files. Papers scattered, forming a blizzard of white and glowing red powder.

"You're going to regret that," he growled, and

blasted her square in the chest with a brilliant circle of purple.

Jacq giggled. "I give up. Don't shoot." She flung down her slingshot and switched on the overhead lights. Looking around, she gasped, torn between amusement and dismay. "We'd better get this place cleaned up before Ebbie comes in."

Mathias collapsed in his chair, shaking yellow powder from his hair. "Don't bother. I'll take care of it if the cleaning crew doesn't."

"I don't mind helping. Besides, I'd feel awful if Ebbie walked in here and saw this. She'd probably faint dead away."

"She almost did the first time she saw what you'd done to my desk." He leaned back and closed his eyes, smiling at the memory. "I had to threaten her with unemployment to keep her from washing it off."

"You did? Really?"

He opened one eye. "I did. Really."

"That was sweet of you." Jacq knelt on the floor and began to gather up the loose paper. "It's almost done, you know. The desk, I mean. I just have one final addition to make and—"

Before she could finish her comment, Mathias catapulted out of his chair. "*Jacq!*"

She looked up, astonished by the harshness of his voice. "What is it? What's wrong?"

"Put the papers down," he ordered tautly. "Just leave them for the cleaning crew, all right?"

Afterward, she couldn't say what tipped her off. She vaguely remembered staring at him, absorbing the intensity of emotion reflected in his eyes. The green turned a shade she'd never seen before and in that moment time slowed, stretched. She recalled shaking her head and whispering, "Oh, no." And then she glanced down and really looked at the papers she held in her hands.

The one on top was yellow—a color she'd always considered sunny and cheerful and rather hopeful. It had been ripped from a legal pad. The heading leaped out at her, written in bold caps. She knew it was Mathias's handwriting. It matched the printing on the reservation card he'd filled out at the Heaven on Earth resort. It read, "Spontaneous Activities Guaranteed To Capture Jack Rabbitt." And there on the paper, carefully numbered, he'd detailed everything they'd done since they'd first met.

She could hear J.J.'s voice cataloguing Mathias's personality traits. *Careful. Exacting. Thorough. Unbelievably precise.*

"I think," she whispered. "I'm going to be sick."

Mathias knelt beside Jacq, easing the papers from her grasp. "Sweetheart, I can explain."

"Please don't touch me," she requested politely.

"Honey, listen."

"I'm a procurement, aren't I?"

"Yes, but—"

"How silly of me not to have realized sooner." A pained laugh escaped. "No wonder you never asked what I did for a living. You already knew, didn't you?"

"I suspected. After you painted the baby dragon on my desk, it confirmed your identity."

She closed her eyes, overwhelmed by the sheer irony of it all. "You want to know something funny?"

"At this point, I think we could really use a bit of levity."

"I painted that dragon out of gratitude for lunch. Remember? You'd had it catered from House Milano. After you left to meet with Patsie and Dana, it occurred to me how I might bring some color into your life." Her laugh took on a harsh edge. "It was my way of thanking you. But instead it trapped me."

"It's not a trap! I set out to procure you for a client. Instead I fell in love. I didn't plan it. It just happened. And it happened the moment I set eyes on you."

"No! I don't believe you."

"Why not? It's the truth."

"The *truth*?" She glared at him, knocking the papers from his grasp. They scattered like autumn leaves before a harsh north wind. "What would you know about the truth? Our entire relationship is based on lies."

"I'm not lying about this."

"How can you expect me to believe anything you have to say? I've been there, remember? Done that."

"I am not Elliott," he stated through gritted teeth.

She lifted an eyebrow. "Oh, really? Tell me... What's the difference? You both had an ulterior motive for romancing me. You both professed to love me. And then you both used me to further your own career. There's only one tiny step left. The one where you take what you want and walk out the door."

"That's not going to happen."

"You're right. It's not. Because I'm walking through that door first."

"Jacq, you've worked with me on a number of procurements. You must know by now that I don't operate like that."

"Don't you?" She picked up the yellow sheet of paper and shook it at him. "It's all here in black and white, Mathias. It's obvious that our dates were a series of tests to determine the best way to approach Jack Rabbitt. Do you deny it?"

"No!" Frustration burned in his gaze. "I can't deny

planning ways to hold your interest. But I'd hoped to find something to offer in exchange for your help. And I figured that if there wasn't anything I could give you, maybe by working with me you'd see that my procurements were well-intentioned. That I try and help people. Do you think I would have used deception if the need wasn't great and the cause just?''

"I don't know what I think anymore." She stood, putting as much distance between them as possible. "Just out of curiosity... What were you going to offer in exchange for my identity?"

His expression closed over. "What I have to offer, you apparently don't want."

"You're right. There's nothing you have that I want." Tears blurred her eyes and she fought to control them. She would not cry. At least not now. Carefully, she removed his ring from her finger and set it on the desk. "I won't be needing this anymore. Maybe the person you procured it from would like it back."

"I didn't procure it. I had a jeweler make it based on your description."

She bit down on her lip, refusing to acknowledge how much his confession meant to her. "Tell your client I'm sorry. It was never my intention to be your first failed procurement."

She'd gotten all the way to the door before she heard his reply.

"Second."

Fury shot through her and she spun in her tracks. "How could you! Don't you dare throw Christopher in my face."

"I wasn't." He rubbed a weary hand across his face. "Go on, Jacq. Leave. I'll tell my client I wasn't able to procure Jack Rabbitt. You're off the hook."

It took every ounce of self-possession to open the door and walk out when what she wanted more than anything was to race across the room and throw herself into his arms. Unfortunately, she'd been down that path before and barely survived the emotional battering. She wouldn't survive again. If she stayed, it would destroy her.

CHAPTER TEN

MATHIAS leaned back in his chair and studied his desk. Jacq's painting was stunning, he thought for the hundredth time. Brilliant, in fact. There was only one minor problem.... She hadn't finished it. Scratching Nemesis behind the ears, he deliberately closed his eyes to shut out the sight. It didn't do any good. The damned thing continued to haunt him.

A knock sounded on the office door and Ebbie walked in. "Good morning, Mr. Blackstone," she said in a disgustingly cheerful voice. "I have the file on the Gravis house. I assume you'll want to sign off on it."

"Put it on the desk, please."

"How did the party go?" she chattered on. "Well, I hope."

"Great."

She carefully placed the file in the tiny section of the desktop not yet painted. "Oh! Ms. Randell left her ring. She must have forgotten it after the party."

With a plaintive meow, Nemesis leaped from Mathias's lap and slipped under the desk. "She didn't forget it."

"She didn't...?" Ebbie cast him a stricken look. "I assume—I assume that means she found out the truth."

"Good assumption."

"And she wouldn't help?" Ebbie questioned, clearly shocked. "I don't believe it. She's worked with you on all those other Christmas procurements, why in the world wouldn't she help with this one?"

''She didn't say. The discussion centered around the fact that I'd deceived her and pretty much stayed there.''

''But once you explained why—''

''We never quite got to the whys and wherefores.''

Ebbie frowned. ''Mathias, didn't you tell her about the Johnsons?''

''She knows about the Johnsons,'' he snapped, surging to his feet and taking up a stance by the windows. He tossed the words over his shoulder. ''I wrote volumes about the Johnsons both to her agent as well as to her publishing company. Apparently none of them give a damn.''

''I don't believe it,'' Ebbie repeated stubbornly. ''Jacq isn't like that. I'm telling you, she doesn't know why you procured her or she wouldn't have returned your ring. You have to talk to her again.''

''And say what?'' He shook his head. ''I did the one thing she couldn't forgive. I lied to her. What's left to discuss?''

Ebbie tilted her chin to a defiant angle. ''I'll tell you what....''

''What do you mean, it's over?'' J.J. stared in disbelief. ''Have you lost your ever-loving mind? You're crazy about him. And Blackstone is crazy about you, too.''

Jacq slouched further down on the couch, throwing an arm across her eyes. ''Correction. He's crazy about Jack Rabbitt.''

J.J. said something short, succinct and painfully rude. ''Okay. So from what you've told me, he initially intended to go after Jack Rabbitt. When his client first approached him that was undoubtedly his plan. But those plans changed at the Limelight reception. From that moment on he wanted you. *You*. Jacq Randell. Not Billie Bunny.''

''Jack Rabbitt. And it was all an act. He pretended to be interested so he could figure out how to procure me for this client of his.''

''You're forgetting something. I was there. As was Cord and Dad. The three of us stood there watching Blackstone watch you. If you'd stuck around a little longer, he'd probably have had you right then and there.''

Jacq glared. ''Don't be crude.''

''Actually, I didn't mean it like that. Interesting that that's how you took it.'' She tilted her head to one side. ''I wonder what would have happened if he'd made his move that night.''

Jacq groaned. No question there. She'd have tumbled into his arms just as readily as she had one week later. She sat up and scowled at her sister. ''What does it matter? The bottom line is—he deceived me. Just like Elliott. He had an ulterior motive for coming on to me. Like Elliott. And he planned to use me. Like Elliott.''

''What if he'd gone after you in a more direct manner? What if he'd knocked on the door of this safe little hideaway of yours and said, 'Hi, there. I'm Mathias Blackstone, procurer extraordinaire, and I want Holly Hare for a client of mine.' How would you have responded?''

''I'd have slammed the door in his face.'' Well... Maybe she'd have kissed him first and then slammed the door.

''My point exactly,'' J.J. said triumphantly. ''So how can you blame him for coming after you in a more circuitous fashion?''

''He didn't have to romance me for his client. He

didn't have to pretend he was spontaneous.'' Tears pricked her eyes. And he certainly didn't have to make love to her.

"Now there's a contradiction for you—using the words Blackstone and spontaneous in the same sentence. That alone should have tipped you off."

"He is spontaneous." Jacq instantly leaped to his defense. "He just has to plan it a little."

J.J. smothered a grin. "Uh-huh. Whatever you say. By the way, who was this client Blackstone tried to procure you for?"

"I don't know," Jacq admitted.

Her sister lifted an eyebrow. "Well, why did his client want to meet Connie Cottontail?"

"Jack Rabbitt. And Mathias never said."

J.J. frowned. "Didn't you ask?"

"We were a little busy shouting at each other," Jacq retorted defensively. "It didn't occur to me to stop mid-scream and ask detailed questions."

"I can understand that. But, what about his other procurements? Can't you get an idea from them?"

"Not really. They're all different."

"Oh, really? Tell me about them. What kinds of things does he procure?"

Jacq shrugged. "Like I said, it varies." She ticked off on her fingers. "He found a painting for Mel. He brought about a meeting between a mother and the child she'd given up for adoption. There were two teenage girls who wanted to find the perfect honeymoon retreat for their parents. I helped him with those as well as the Operation Toys program—"

"You mean that Christmas party you threw?"

"Right."

"The one where he dressed up as Santa Claus for a

bunch of kids even though he'd lost his own son not so long ago?''

Jacq had trouble meeting her sister's eyes. "Yes."

"In other words, his job is to fulfill wishes. Good wishes. Beneficial wishes."

"Not all of them are beneficial," Jacq insisted. "He has one client who wants to buy a house belonging to this sweet little old lady."

"And Mathias stole it from her? Threatened her? Turned her out into the street?"

"Not yet." Jacq glowered. "But there's plenty of time. He still has four days until Christmas."

"You're right." J.J. leaped to her feet and began to pace. "I'll just bet he's gonna go over there on Christmas Eve, drag the woman out by her graying bun and chuck poor granny and all her stuff into the gutter. The bastard."

Jacq gave a reluctant laugh. "Okay. Maybe he won't do that."

"Oh, no?" J.J. questioned gently. "Why not?"

"Because he's hoping to find a way to satisfy both parties." Jacq bowed her head. "It's sort of a thing with him."

"A thing. You mean, like a principle or something?"

"I guess you could say that."

"Uh-huh."

"You think I'm wrong, don't you?"

"I think maybe you'd better find out why Mathias wanted to find Jack Rabbitt so badly," J.J. suggested softly. "There must have been a very powerful reason to make him forego his principles enough to deceive you."

"He's not Elliott, is he?" Jacq whispered, stating what she already knew in her heart.

"No, Jacq. He's not."

Why, oh why, hadn't she realized that sooner? Jacq wondered in despair. And now that she had... Was it too late to make things right? There was only one way to find out. She leaped to her feet.

She had to talk to Mathias. Now.

Jacq opened the smoked-glass door marked "Blackstone," fighting to remain calm. Her grip tightened on her satchel of paints but for the first time ever, the familiar clatter of jars did nothing to reassure her. Ebbie sat behind her desk and looked up, surprise and relief written all over her expressive features.

"Oh, Ms. Randell. Thank heavens you're here."

"I'm sorry it's taken so long for me to come to my senses," Jacq said contritely. "Is Mathias in? I'd like to see him."

Ebbie shook her head. "He's visiting a client."

"Oh." Jacq nibbled on her lip and thought fast. "I wonder if I could ask a favor."

"Of course."

"Do you think he'd object if I finished the painting on his desk?"

"I think it would mean a lot to him." The secretary hesitated and then removed a folder from her drawer. "And would you mind leaving this for him? He'll want to see it when he returns."

"Sure." Jacq accepted the file and started toward the office.

Outside the set of black double doors she paused long enough to draw a deep breath. Then she shoved them open and strode into the darkened room. She switched on the light nearest his desk and started to put the folder on his chair when she noticed the name on the tab.

Jack Rabbitt.

There was no doubt that Ebbie had given her the file for a reason. Slowly Jacq flipped it open and began to read.

There was a lot of general information detailing his search—all very precise and thorough and methodical. Typical of Mathias, she thought with a reluctant smile. She turned the pages, delving deeper. Next came months' worth of correspondence between Mathias and her agent and editor. Mathias's letters were a long string of requests to meet with the author and illustrator known as Jack Rabbitt and the reason behind his request. The reason left her stunned. And in response were an equal number of letters in reply. Each was polite, though adamant, in refusing his request, explaining they were legally bound to maintain Jack Rabbitt's confidentiality. The author refused to even discuss the subject of a personal appearance.

Tears filled her eyes. Every word was true, just as every word condemned her. No wonder Mathias had chosen to approach her the way he had. She wiped the moisture from her cheeks and turned to the very last page in the file—the damning sheet of yellow legal paper.

She read it for a second time, giving it more attention than she had before. Why hadn't she noticed how much thought he'd put into the activities he'd chosen? It must have been very difficult to open himself, to allow an outsider such an intimate peek into his life. She drew a shaken breath. But he'd done it anyway, because his client's need outweighed his own. Something had been written on the back of the paper. She flipped it over and saw it was another list.

Only this one read, "Reasons Why Jacq Should Marry

Me." The column of "cons" ran the full length of the page and some of the itemized notations nearly broke her heart. He was too rigid, too black-and-white. Too grid-oriented. He'd hurt her by exposing her secret. He lacked spontaneity. He'd steal the color from her world and give nothing in return. On the opposite side were the "pros."

There was only one.

I love her, he'd scrawled in a heavy hand.

It took a long time before she'd composed herself enough to complete the painting. As she worked she wondered how Mathias would respond when he saw it—and how he'd answer the question she left there. Nemesis came by at one point to watch her work.

"You and Angelica had better get along, that's all I can say," she muttered. "Would you like a companion?"

To her relief, Nemesis gave a reassuring purr.

Half an hour later all that remained was one final detail. Her signature. Then she picked up the phone and called home.

"Turk Randell," her father answered brusquely.

"It's me."

"You sound odd, Jacq. Is everything all right?"

"Not really." She wound the telephone cord around her finger. "Dad... I need your help."

There was a long moment of silence. And then in a voice heavy with emotion, Turk said, "I've waited three and half long years to hear you say that. Tell me what you need and it's yours."

Mathias strode into his office, exhaustion riding him hard. He'd gone to visit the Johnsons personally and it had been a painful meeting. Nemesis sat in his chair behind the desk and meowed a greeting. Crossing to give the cat a scratch, Mathias glanced automatically at Jacq's painting.

"My, God," he muttered beneath his breath. "She finished it. She actually finished it."

The two dragons still held center stage—only the male's eyes were no longer wary. Instead it was the female's expression that held a question. Shafts of gold-flecked sunlight pierced the surrounding jungle and poured down toward the pair without quite reaching them. Something danced within the golden light and it took Mathias a few minutes to realize what it was. Dragons. Four infant dragons. And while the male dragon still held a decidedly wretched rat beneath one claw, he reached toward the light with the other. Reached toward the children with a beseeching look in his green eyes. And where the light touched the black of his scales, they glowed, glittering with all the colors in the rainbow.

He never knew how long he sat there or how long it took him to notice that one last detail. Even after he'd spotted it, he still didn't immediately understand the significance. But once it dawned on him, he shot to his feet and bolted for the door.

In the most revealing gesture of all, she'd signed the painting Jacq Randell instead of using her pseudonym.

Jacq poked her head around the doorway of the hospital room and smiled at the young girl she found there. "Hi," she said with a friendly grin.

Huge dark eyes stared curiously at her for a moment and then a hesitant smile slipped across the seven-year-old's pale face. "Hello."

"Are you Tosha Johnson?" Jacq asked, stepping into the room.

"Yes." Wariness crept into her gaze. "Are you a doctor?"

Jacq shook her head. "I write books and I understand you wanted to meet me. My name's Jacq. Jack Rabbitt."

Tosha's reaction was heart-breaking. A look of radiant joy spread over her delicate features and she grasped the sheet so tightly her fingers turned white. "I wished and wished for you to come and visit me. Everybody said no. They said you wouldn't come. But I knew you would. I just knew it."

"I—" Jacq swallowed hard, painfully aware of how close she'd come to destroying this little girl's dreams. She held out the gift she'd brought. "Merry Christmas."

"What's that?"

"Something I brought for you."

Slowly Tosha took the package, studying the cheery wrapping paper and huge floppy bow in stunned silence. Finally, she asked, "May I open it?"

"I wish you would. Do you mind if I sit down for a minute?"

"Sure. My mom will be back soon. Do you want to use her chair?"

"I'd like that. Thanks." While Tosha carefully unwrapped the present, Jacq took a seat and removed her sketch pad, paints and brushes from her satchel.

"Oh! It's one of your books." She hugged it to her chest. "Thank you."

"You're very welcome. Take a look inside."

Tosha opened the book and blinked in surprise. "You wrote my name and signed it and everything."

"You're the only one I've ever done that for."

"Wait until all my friends see." She looked uncertainly at Jacq. "Do you think they'll believe it was really you? Maybe they'll say I made it up."

"They'll believe you. I promise." Jacq rested her sketch pad on her knee. "Tell me something, Tosha. Who's your favorite character in my books?"

"The fairies," she replied promptly. "I like them best because they're so pretty and they can fly anywhere they want." She regarded Jacq curiously. "Are you going to make a painting?"

"I sure am. I'm going to make a painting just for you."

The gratitude that lit Tosha's eyes was humbling. Jacq swallowed against the knot in her throat and determinedly set to work. The next few hours were a delight with the two of them laughing and talking about everything from school to pets to favorite TV shows. At one point Tosha nodded off and her mother returned. Jacq introduced herself and Michelle Johnson promptly burst into tears.

"I didn't think Mathias would be able to pull it off. He said he'd tried everything and couldn't find you."

Jacq blinked hard. "It's Christmas," she responded lightly. "It's the time for miracles."

"Tosha's going to need more than one, I'm afraid."

"She has to have a bone marrow transplant, doesn't she?" At Michelle's nod, Jacq asked, "Have they found a donor, yet?"

"No. It's her genetic makeup that's making it so difficult. Mathias had the same problem with Christopher because Lisa had such an interesting heritage."

"Christopher had leukemia?" Jacq questioned in distress.

"Didn't Mathias tell you? You see, minorities are the most difficult of all to match and Tosha has a bit of everything. West Indian, African-American, even Native American Indian.''

''I wonder… Perhaps a public appeal will help,'' Jacq suggested diffidently.

''We've tried that.'' Michelle's shoulders slumped in defeat. ''There was an article or two in the local newspapers, a brief flurry of responses. And then nothing.''

''I'm thinking along the lines of a national appeal.''

Michelle stared blankly. ''National? Why would anyone give Tosha's situation national publicity? She's just one of thousands of similar cases.''

Jacq blushed. ''Well… They wouldn't if it were Tosha alone, more's the shame. But maybe Jack Rabbitt could pull a string or two. My father owns a PR firm and if you don't object, we'll use my name to draw attention to Tosha's plight. I have to warn you, it could mean a lot of media attention. That can be pretty overwhelming if you're not used to it.''

''It would also mean helping a lot of people just like Tosha,'' Michelle said slowly.

Jacq nodded. ''Yes, it would.''

''But…'' Michelle fought back a resurgence of tears. ''Are you sure you want to do that? You'd have to reveal your identity. Mathias said it was really important for you to keep it a secret.''

Jacq shrugged. ''Helping Tosha is more important.''

At the sound of her name, the little girl stirred. Her lashes fluttered and she opened her eyes, smiling when she saw Jacq. ''You're still here.''

''I sure am. And look what I have for you.'' She held up the painting she'd completed. ''It's still wet, but as soon as it dries, it's all yours.''

''Mommy! Mommy, look! I'm a fairy.''

Michelle smiled in wonder. ''I see that, sweetie.''

"How'd you like to be in my next book?" Jacq offered.

Tosha's eyes widened. "Can I? Will you let me?"

Jacq nodded. "I promise. All you have to do is work real hard at getting well."

Color blossomed across Tosha's cheekbones. "Will you make me a fairy again?"

"Absolutely. I'll even give you a dragon for a playmate."

"A baby dragon?" a voice asked from the doorway.

Jacq spun around with a silent gasp and met Mathias's impassive gaze with a hint of trepidation.

"Well?" he prompted, leaning against the door frame. "Will it be a baby dragon?"

Uncertainty filled her. Obviously he'd seen the changes she'd made to the desk. But how did he feel about it? "I think that's up to you. Baby dragons need a lot of sunlight in order to survive."

"And color?"

"That, too."

"Then that's what we'll have to give them. Won't we?"

It was all the answer she needed. With an inarticulate cry, she flew into his welcoming arms. They remained with Tosha for another hour before making reluctant farewells, promising to return again in the morning. And then they were in his car, speeding northward through Seattle. Jacq wasn't the least surprised when Mathias eventually stopped at the park above Shilshole Bay. It looked far different than the last time they'd visited, though. The Olympic Mountains were well hidden behind a bank of heavy gray clouds and the Sound boiled with choppy waves.

"You haven't asked me about Adele Gravis or her house," he commented as they left the car.

She sent him a quick sidelong glance. "You mean your first failed procurement?"

"Ebbie told you?" he asked wryly.

"No, she didn't. I worked it out for myself. I can even guess how you resolved the situation."

He lifted an eyebrow. "You can, huh?"

She leaned against the fence at the edge of the bluff and nodded. "If I were a betting woman, I'd lay odds Adele has three brand new boarders. And I'd also bet they all play a mean game of bridge."

He shook his head in admiration. "How'd you figure that out?"

She gave him a smug grin. "Simple. It's exactly what I would have done. How did your client take it?"

"He was disappointed, but not surprised. We're looking at other houses." Mathias hesitated a minute, then asked, "Why did you do it?"

"Go and visit Tosha?" He nodded and she admitted, "I realized you weren't the only one living in the shadows. I was, too. And I decided I'd been there long enough."

"Life's to be lived, is that it?"

"Something along those lines." Snow flurries filled the air, driven by a cold northwestern wind. Mathias opened the front of his coat and Jacq stepped into the warm haven of his arms. She sighed in delight as he closed the heavy wool around them. "I've asked Dad to arrange for an auction. I'm going to sell one of my paintings and donate the proceeds to the National Marrow Donor Program. I'm hoping the resulting publicity will help find a match for Tosha."

"Not bad for your first solo procurement. Which painting are you going to auction off?"

Jacq grinned. "The one with the fairy riding a butterfly."

A quiet laugh rumbled through his chest. "J.J.'s going to kill you when she finds out."

"It's her own fault. She's the one who convinced me to give you a second chance."

He glanced down at her. "Did you need much convincing?"

"Not much," she confessed, wrapping her arms more tightly about his waist. "I'm sorry, Mathias. I had no idea you were trying to get hold of Jack Rabbitt for such an important reason. Neither my editor nor my agent ever approached me about it. And that's my fault, too. I'd made it clear that I didn't want to know about any of the requests they might receive. It didn't occur to me that some of them might be for such vital causes."

"Ebbie suggested that might be the case." He rested his chin on top of her head and sighed. "I've spent a very long time looking for you, Ms. Rabbitt. You've proved to be one tough bunny to snare."

"A long time?" Three months wasn't long. Not long at all. And then it clicked and the pain hit so hard she had trouble catching her breath. "Oh, no. Oh, no," she whispered over and over before dissolving into tears. "*Christopher*! I was Christopher's first request, wasn't I? The one you couldn't fulfill."

He didn't bother with denials. He just held on to her, rocking her until she'd regained her composure enough to speak.

"You must hate me," she said in a tired voice.

"I could never hate you." He cupped her face, forcing her to meet his impassioned gaze. "I love you, Jacq. I fell in love with you three years ago, when I held my son each night and read your first book to him. I fell in love with your joy for life and your spirit and the sweetness of your stories. And then the first time I saw you, I fell even harder.''

''You couldn't have known what I was like. Not enough to—''

''I knew. It was there for me to see. All I had to do was look. That night at the Davenports's I realized I'd found my other half. I knew I'd found the one woman who could make me whole again.'' He reached into his pocket and retrieved her ring. ''Will you marry me, Jacq? A real engagement, this time?''

Tears glittered on the ends of her lashes. ''Do you suppose there's still time for a Christmas wedding?''

''If not, we can hold it on New Year's Day. I can't think of a better time to start a new life together.''

A hint of mischief replaced her tears. ''It would still give us time to have our first baby by Halloween.''

''Especially if we get started right away.''

And then he lowered his head and kissed her. It was a kiss of hope and determination, of sunshine and color. Of trust and faith and renewal. It was a promise for the future. But most of all it was a kiss of love.

LIMELIGHT INTERNATIONAL: PRESS RELEASE

Jack Rabbitt's fifteenth book, *Celebration*, is just that. A celebration. And with good cause. Devoted readers may remember young Tosha Johnson, the seven-year-old girl in desperate need of a bone marrow transplant to cure her leukemia. Her plight prompted Jack Rabbitt to come out of hiding and make a national appeal for donors—an appeal that resulted in a successful match for young Tosha!

Well, *Celebration* is dedicated to young Tosha—in honor of her thirteenth birthday! Happy Birthday, Tosha! With your leukemia cured, we're certain you'll celebrate many, many more.

EPILOGUE

JACQ'S first baby didn't arrive by Halloween as they'd hoped. Instead, their son was born on Thanksgiving Day. He was every bit as happy and healthy as they could have wished and had Mathias's dark hair and Jacq's bright hazel eyes.

As the years progressed, Mathias never forgot the tragedy of his first son's death. But he did find the love he'd thought forever lost to him. He found it in the faces of the children he ultimately raised and in the eyes of the woman he loved most in all the world. And he found it grew with each day, its intensity banishing the few remaining shadows.

He never did replace his dragon desk, instead he protected it with a glass cover. Over time, it became as well-known as Jacq's books and he displayed it proudly to visitors from all over the world. Only three final changes were made to the desk before it was deemed completed.

The questioning expression in the female dragon's eyes turned to contentment and joy.

The name ''Blackstone'' was added to Jacq's signature.

And infant dragons frolicking at their parents' feet.

There were four altogether. Two boys and two girls, just as Mathias had promised.

Each year thousands of children and adults are diagnosed with life-threatening blood diseases like leukemia. For many the only cure will be a bone marrow transplant. Approximately 70 percent of those who need a marrow donor will have to search a donor registry for a match. Minorities have the most difficult time identifying a life-saving match. It's especially crucial for people of diverse backgrounds to join their National Registry. It could mean the difference between life and death for a searching patient. If you would like to help please call for more information.

In the United States call the
National Marrow Donor Program
1-800-MARROW-2
1 800-627-7692

In Canada call the Canadian Red Cross Society
1-800-668-2866

Coming in August 1997!

THE BETTY NEELS RUBY COLLECTION

August 1997—Stars Through the Mist
September 1997—The Doubtful Marriage
October 1997—The End of the Rainbow
November 1997—Three for a Wedding
December 1997—Roses for Christmas
January 1998—The Hasty Marriage

COLLECTOR'S EDITION

This August start assembling the
Betty Neels Ruby Collection. Six of the
most requested and best-loved titles have
been especially chosen for this collection.
From August 1997 until January 1998,
one title per month will be available to avid
fans. Spot the collection by the lush ruby red
cover with the gold Collector's Edition banner
and your favorite author's name—Betty Neels!

Available in August at your favorite retail outlet.

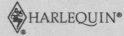

HARLEQUIN®

ℋarlequin Romance®

SIMPLY THE BEST

*Authors you'll treasure,
books you'll want to keep!*

Harlequin Romance books just keep getting better
and better...and we're delighted to continue with our
Simply the Best showcase for 1997, highlighting a
special author each month!

These are romances we know you'll love reading—
more than once! Because they are,
quite simply, the best....

**November 1997—
DANIEL AND DAUGHTER (#3480)
by Lucy Gordon**

and for Christmas...

**December 1997—
HER SECRET SANTA (#3486)
by Day Leclaire**

Available in November and December wherever
Harlequin books are sold. And watch out for more
exciting new miniseries in 1998!

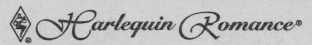

Harlequin Romance®

Invites You to A Wedding!

Whirlwind Weddings
Combines the heady romance of a whirlwind courtship with the excitement of a wedding—strong heroes, feisty heroines and marriages made not so much in heaven as in a hurry!

What's the catch? All our heroes and heroines meet and marry within a week! Mission impossible? Well, a lot can happen in seven days....

January 1998—#3487 MARRY IN HASTE
by Heather Allison

February 1998—#3491 DASH TO THE ALTAR
by Ruth Jean Dale

March 1998—#3495 THE TWENTY-FOUR-HOUR BRIDE
by Day Leclaire

April 1998—#3499 MARRIED IN A MOMENT
by Jessica Steele

Who says you can't hurry love?

Available wherever Harlequin books are sold.

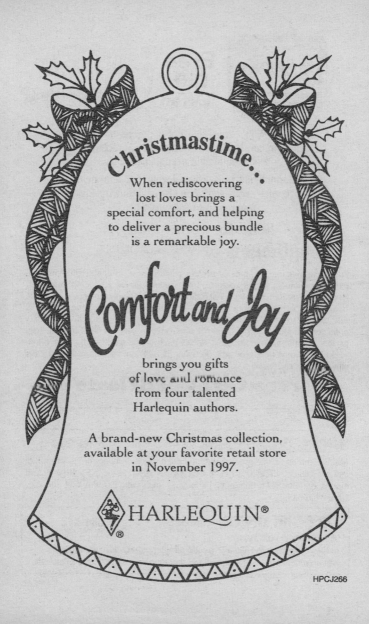

Free Gift Offer

With a Free Gift proof-of-purchase
from any Harlequin® book, you can receive
a beautiful cubic zirconia pendant.

This stunning marquise-shaped stone is a genuine cubic
zirconia—accented by an 18" gold tone necklace.
(Approximate retail value $19.95)

Send for yours today...
compliments of HARLEQUIN®

To receive your free gift, a cubic zirconia pendant, send us one original proof-of-purchase, photocopies not accepted, from the back of any Harlequin Romance®, Harlequin Presents®, Harlequin Temptation®, Harlequin Superromance®, Harlequin Intrigue®, Harlequin American Romance®, or Harlequin Historicals® title available at your favorite retail outlet, together with the Free Gift Certificate, plus a check or money order for $1.65 U.S./$2.15 CAN. (do not send cash) to cover postage and handling, payable to Harlequin Free Gift Offer. We will send you the specified gift. Allow 6 to 8 weeks for delivery. Offer good until December 31, 1997, or while quantities last. Offer valid in the U.S. and Canada only.

Free Gift Certificate

Name: _____

Address: _____

City: _____ State/Province: _____ Zip/Postal Code: _____

Mail this certificate, one proof-of-purchase and a check or money order for postage and handling to: HARLEQUIN FREE GIFT OFFER 1997. In the U.S.: 3010 Walden Avenue, P.O. Box 9071, Buffalo NY 14269-9057. In Canada: P.O. Box 604, Fort Erie, Ontario L2Z 5X3.

FREE GIFT OFFER   084-KEZ

ONE PROOF-OF-PURCHASE
To collect your fabulous FREE GIFT, a cubic zirconia pendant, you must include this
original proof-of-purchase for each gift with the properly completed Free Gift Certificate.

084-KEZR